George
and the
Goblin Hole

Professor Watermelon

Illustrated By: Josh Smart

DEDICATION

For my George and his Granny – P.W.

For Andy-andy-bo-bandy-banana-fana-fo-fandy-fe-fy-mo-mandy-ANDY! – J.S.

James Whitcomb Riley (1849-1916) is photographed with Lockerbie (his beloved poodle) and the descendants of the Indianapolis German Club. This photograph was taken in front of Mr. Riley's Lockerbie home in 1915 in preparation for the Indiana Centennial celebration.

Dear Reader,

This book is a tribute to James Whitcomb Riley and his beloved poodle, Lockerbie. Dennis Ewing, the former butler of 528 Lockerbie Street, is also celebrated throughout these pages.

While I refer to these real historical figures of Indiana History, the story itself is fiction and from my own imagination.

Several of Mr. Riley's poems are also used in this story to drive and thicken the plot. Mr. Riley wrote most of these poems in Hoosier Dialect, the way people from Indiana spoke in the 1800's. For example, the word "children" was spoken as "childern".

And I hope you love a good GHOST story made complete with GOBLINS, because that's exactly what you have in your hands.

BOO!

Did I scare you?

Good! Now, sit back, relax, and enjoy a new Hoosier tale.

Happy Indiana Bicentennial!

Professor Watermelon

P.S. After reading this book, take a tour of the REAL James Whitcomb Riley Museum Home in Indianapolis. The REAL Judy might be your tour guide (wink).

Chapter 1

George waited patiently behind the curtains. His right hand was in his pocket rubbing the moonstone that his grandma had given to him. She said it would soothe his nerves and give him courage, but George wasn't so sure.

He had never spoken in front of such a large crowd of people, and these weren't just any people. They were his fellow students at James Whitcomb Riley Elementary. If he had known that this was a requirement of joining the 4th

Grade Poetry Club, he would've never signed up. He would've kept his fondness of rhythms and rhymes to himself.

George could hear the squeaky hinges on the theatre seats each time a student sat down. And with each squeak, George's mouth got drier and drier. And to say there were butterflies in his stomach would be putting it lightly. Pelicans would be more like it – clumsy, large-billed pelicans!

Mr. Irvington, the principal, took the microphone and walked in front of the curtain. He was a very tall and skinny man who wore only brown suits and always smelled like salty potato chips.

"Boys and girls, may I have you attention?" he said. "Today is Poet's Day."

He brushed his lapels free from crumbs. "Our school is named after Indiana's most famous poet – James Whitcomb Riley."

The crowd was abnormally quiet with only a few whispers of teachers who were directing late arrivals.

"Because our school is named after James Whitcomb Riley," said Mr. Irvington, "it is our tradition to reserve the last day of school before summer break for Poet's Day. And to kick-off this special day, the Fourth Grade Poetry Club will recite some of Mr. Riley's beloved poems. Without further ado, here is Mrs. Woodruff, the poetry club advisor."

Mrs. Woodruff was the exact opposite of Mr. Irvington. She was short and squat and never wore brown. But as for color, she had plenty. For starters, her hair was dark purple, and her cat-eye glasses were orange. She wore more jewelry on her ears, neck and hands than all the ladies on the Home Shopping Channel combined. Her shoe color always matched her nail color, and she wore a different silk scarf for each day of the year.

"Good morning," she said in an exaggerated and dignified tone.

The auditorium stayed silent.

"Good morning!" she said even louder.

After a few more times, the audience finally responded adequately enough for Mrs. Woodruff to continue.

"Welcome to our annual Riley Recital," she said. "My students have been memorizing some very special poetry for you. But first, I want to know how many of you have seen the musical *Annie*. Raise your hands."

Every student, except maybe three, raised their hands. George had seen the musical too, but only on television. The old version, starring Carol Burnett, had come on after dinner one evening. He had no idea who Carol Burnett was, but his grandma had explained that she was a comedic icon, and after watching the musical, George agreed.

"Splendid," said Mrs. Woodruff. "And do you know that 'Annie' would NOT exist if it weren't for our poet, James Whitcomb Riley?"

That was George's cue. His palms instantly moistened, and his moonstone felt slippery in his hand. That didn't matter though. He rubbed it anyway and walked out on stage with Mrs. Woodruff.

"When Riley was a young boy - about the age of George here, a girl came to live with his family. Her name was Mary Alice Smith," lectured Mrs. Woodruff. "She was hired to help Mrs. Riley with the cooking and the cleaning."

Leave it to a first grader to shout out, "Why?"

Mrs. Woodruff smiled at the little girl and then turned to George. "Please tell her, George."

George was barely prepared to recite poetry. He had no idea a "Q and A" session would precede his performance. His cheeks got hotter than they already were.

"Um, well," he stammered. "Mr. Riley's dad was away fighting in the Civil War. Mary Alice Smith was given room and board to help…"

"What's room and board?" the same little girl shouted.

"That meant that she could live at their house and eat their food," said George, "but she had to earn her keep by helping with the chores and stuff." He was surprised that he was able to answer so quickly.

When George could tell that the girl was satisfied, he continued. "After Allie (that's what they called her) finished with her chores, she would tell the Riley kids stories about ghosts and goblins."

This roused the audience. Many students shifted in their seats, and George could hear several "oohs" and "aahs".

"Mr. Riley loved Allie so much that he wrote a poem about her many years later. Allie's name was changed to 'Annie' in this poem."

Mrs. Woodruff took the microphone from George's hand. "Thank you, George, for that wonderful explanation. Are you all ready to hear Mr. Riley's most famous poem, 'Little Orphant Annie'?"

The children yelled a collective, "Yes!"

George took the microphone in one hand and rubbed his moonstone in the other. His nerves had actually settled some, so much that he could feel his knees unlocking. He knew this was a good thing. He had once watched a girl pass out and fall off the risers at the Spring Choir Jubilee. Come to find out, she had locked her knees. An ambulance was called and everything.

"Little Orphant Annie!" George stated the title of the poem.

Just then, a man with a cane and top hat walked into the auditorium and sat down in the very back row, closest to the aisle. He was too far away to get a good look at, but the man resembled...

"No!" said George. "It can't be!"

Mrs. Woodruff had taken a seat next to Mr. Irvington in the front row. They both gave George a puzzled look and then looked back to where George was staring and pointing. Everyone else turned to look at what was causing the distraction.

"James Whitcomb Riley!" said George more loudly this time. "He's sitting right there. Can't you see him?"

That's when George's palms dried up, his mouth moistened and his voice boomed.

Little Orphant Annie's come to our house to stay,
An' wash the cups an' saucers up, an' brush the crumbs away,
An' shoo the chickens off the porch, an' dust the hearth, an' sweep,
An' make the fire, an' bake the bread, an' earn her board-an-keep;
An' all us other childern, when the supper-things is done,
We set around the kitchen fire an' has the mostest fun,
A-listenin' to the witch-tales 'at Annie tells about,
An' the Gobble-uns 'at gits you
Ef you
Don't
Watch
Out!

Wunst they wuz a little boy wouldn't say his prayers,
An' when he went to bed at night, away up-stairs,
His Mammy heerd him holler, an' his Daddy heerd him bawl,
An' when they turn't the kivvers down, he wuzn't there at all!
An' they seeked him in the rafter-room, an' cubby-hole, an' press,
An seeked him up the chimbly-flue, an' ever'-wheres, I guess;
But all they ever found wuz thist his pants an' roundabout,
An' the Gobble-uns 'll git you
Ef you

Don't
Watch
Out!

An' one time a little girl 'ud allus laugh an' grin,
An' make fun of ever' one, an' all her blood-an'-kin;
An' wunst, when they was "company," an' ole folks wuz there,
She mocked 'em an' shocked 'em, an' said she didn't care!
An' thist as she kicked her heels, an' turn't to run an' hide,
They wuz two great big Black Things a-standin' by her side,
An' they snatched her through the ceilin' 'for she knowed what she's
about!
An' the Gobble-uns 'll git you
Ef you
Don't
Watch
Out!

An' little Orphant Annie says, when the blaze is blue,
An' the lamp-wick sputters, an' the wind goes woo-oo!
An' you hear the crickets quit, an' the moon is gray,
An' the lightnin'bugs in dew is all squenched away,
You better mind yer parunts, an' yer teachurs fond an' dear,
An' churish them 'at loves you, an' dry the orphant's tear,
An' he'p the pore an' needy ones 'at clusters all about,
Er the Gobble-uns 'll git you
Ef you
Don't
Watch
Out!

The whole auditorium erupted with applause, and as they were clapping, the man stood, tipped his top hat at George, and exited the theatre.

Chapter 2

"That was a great act," said Mrs. Woodruff, when they got back to the classroom. "For a second, I thought James Whitcomb Riley was back from the dead!"

George didn't respond. He didn't want to tell his teachers and friends that he actually DID see Mr. Riley sitting in the back row. They would probably call an ambulance for him and request a mental evaluation. But George was confident, and he knew that what he saw was real.

The rest of Poet's Day, George couldn't focus.
Librarians came in from the Indianapolis Public Library to
promote their Summer Reading Program, but George
couldn't even listen. Their words funneled in and out of his
brain faster than water down a drain.

As he walked home, he was almost hit by a car while
crossing 38th Street. He didn't hear the crossing guard
blow her whistle, and he barely felt her tugging him to
safety.

"You almost got us both killed," she said, once they
were back on the sidewalk. "Get your head out of the
clouds, young man!"

George apologized to the crossing guard and gave
himself a little slap on the face to bring himself back to
reality. He walked the rest of the way home down Dr.
Martin Luther King, Jr. Street with no problems. When he
reached his front porch, he sat down at the top step and
stared across the street.

"How come you sittin' out there by yourself?" asked
Granny through the screen door. "You better get in here
and eat these cookies."

That was one way to snap George back to the present.
"Snickerdoodles?" he said.

"Snickerdoodles," said Granny.

George took off his baseball cap and dropped it and his
backpack onto his dad's recliner. He followed Granny to
the kitchen.

"But you can't have any until you tell me about your
recital," she said, blocking the doorway with her body.

Granny was a small framed lady, but she had the
strength of a tiger. Fortunately, she wouldn't need to use
that strength since the smell of hot cinnamon and butter
was enough to make George spill any information she
wanted.

"My performance was good," said George, inching closer to the kitchen doorway. "My teacher even said so."

"Good," said Granny. "The moonstone worked."

"Yeah," agreed George. "I think it also brought Mr. Riley back from the dead."

Granny stepped backwards into the kitchen, allowing space for George to pass. He sat down at the kitchen table and waited as Granny opened the oven door and pulled out the first batch of snickerdoodles. She sat them on the top of the stove to cool.

"Now, what's this about a ghost?" she said. "Usually amethysts attract ghosts, not moonstones."

"Well, I saw him as clearly as I see you," said George.

"What did he look like?"

"Just like the picture in the hallway at school," said George. "Top hat, cane, and fancy old-man-clothes."

Granny laughed. "Kind of like my fancy old lady clothes?" she said swishing around in her vibrant pink and yellow flowery housecoat.

"Those are the only clothes you wear," said George. "Do you even wash them?"

"Child, I oughta smack your head," she said. "I have seven house coats —one for each day of the week. You know that."

Granny was George's paternal grandmother. She never left her house, except for doctor appointments and Easter service. She was sixty-two years old and had lived in the same house on MLK Street since she was twenty-three. George and his dad had lived with her since he was in kindergarten. That was the year his mom had died.

"Hey, good lookin'," said a man's voice from the family room.

"See?" said Granny. "Somebody thinks I'm fancy."

"Granny made snickerdoodles!" said George.

"I smelled them all the way across the street," said Mr. Ewing.

Granny's house was right across from America's third largest cemetery, Crown Hill. And George's dad was a groundskeeper there. Sometimes he even helped dig the graves.

"George was just telling me about his poetry recital," said Granny, putting a plate of snickerdoodles on the kitchen table, "and how he saw a ghost."

"A ghost?" said Mr. Ewing, smirking.

"Granny, you weren't supposed to say anything," said George with his mouth already full.

"No secrets in this house," she said, handing a cookie to her son. "Isn't that right, Denny?"

"Rule number one since I was knee high to a cricket," he agreed.

Taking his second snickerdoodle, George told his father the whole story. By the time he finished, the cookies were gone.

"I believe every word, son," said Mr. Ewing. "I've seen a few things that I can't explain while mowing around all those graves. Matter of fact, I saw a little green girl at Riley's tomb once.

Both George and Granny laughed out loud.

"What?" said Mr. Ewing. "We can believe in ghosts around here but not little green people?"

"Okay, kids. That's enough." said Granny. Even though Mr. Ewing was thirty-four-years-old, she still called them both kids. "Here's another plate of cookies. Save room for Big Momma BLT's tonight."

Big Momma BLT's were sandwiches of epic proportions. Granny made them with three pieces of bread and two layers of bacon, tomato and lettuce. George ate his with honey-mustard sauce. They were heaven on Earth, unless you were the pig.

George grabbed two more snickerdoodles and headed upstairs to read. He read at least an hour every night – sometimes three. His mom had been a preschool teacher and had taught him to read before he was five years old. His favorite memories of his mother were of the two of them reading together.

A bookshelf covered an entire wall of George's room. Most of the books had come from his mother's collection. She had hundreds of picture books that had been in her classroom. "Mrs. Wendy Ewing" was written on the inside of each cover. George would often find himself tracing his mother's handwriting with his finger. It made him feel as if she was still right there with him.

Now that he was going into fifth grade, he had begun reading the classic Newberry winners like *Bud, Not Buddy* by Christopher Paul Curtis and *Dear Mr. Henshaw* by Beverly Cleary. Currently, he was reading *Sounder* by William H. Armstrong.

George loved dogs, and *Sounder* was about a boy and his dog. Better yet, the boy was African American just like him. It was often hard for George to find books with main characters that looked like him. That didn't keep him from reading other great books about other great kids, but it was extra special when he found main characters with brown skin.

George was in the middle of chapter eleven when his concentration was broken by an important recollection. He needed his dad to sign a permission slip. School was out for the summer, but Mrs. Woodruff had promised to take the poetry club to the James Whitcomb Riley Museum Home. They were supposed to go the previous Monday, but the museum had to cancel due to "unforeseen circumstances". Luckily, Mrs. Woodruff called a few days later and the lady who answered the phone invited the group down the following Saturday – the first day of summer vacation.

Since they would be taking a school bus, a permission slip was due. Everyone was supposed to meet in the school's parking lot at 9:30am. How strange it would be to wake up early on a Saturday and go to school, but George was excited to see the museum. And maybe he could pull the tour guide aside and ask about any ghost sightings in the house.

The smell of fried bacon wafted up the stairs, pulling George from his bed and down to the kitchen. Supper was on the table

Chapter 3

George felt the tires bounce over the cobblestones as soon as the school bus made its last turn onto Lockerbie Street.

"Here we are, children," said Mrs. Woodruff. She wore a teal and gold scarf that matched her nails and shoes. "This is Lockerbie Street, the street made famous by one of Mr. Riley's poems. Sarah, would you do the honors?"

As the bus's breaks screeched to a halt in front of the museum, Sarah St. Clair took a deep breath and smiled at the other seven children of the poetry club. Sarah was one of those kids who always had to be the best at everything. She was on the math bowl and spell bowl teams. She made straight A's, and she already knew how to play six instruments, including the pipe organ. George had wondered who wakes up one morning and decides that they are going to learn the pipe organ.

And without skipping a line, word or beat, Sarah recited the poem Lockerbie Street.

Such a dear little street it is, nestled away
From the noise of the city and heat of the day,
In cool shady coverts of whispering trees,
With their leaves lifted up to shake hands with the breeze
Which in all its wide wanderings never may meet
With a resting-place fairer than Lockerbie street!
There is such a relief, from the clangor and din
Of the heart of the town, to go loitering in
Through the dim, narrow walks, with the sheltering shade
Of the trees waving over the long promenade,
And littering lightly the ways of our feet
With the gold of the sunshine of Lockerbie street.
And the nights that come down the dark pathways of dusk,
With the stars in their tresses, and odors of musk
In their moon-woven raiments, bespangled with dews,
And looped up with lilies for lovers to use
In the songs that they sing to the tinkle and beat
Of their sweet serenadings through Lockerbie street.
O my Lockerbie street! You are fair to be seen—
Be it noon of the day, or the rare and serene
Afternoon of the night-- you are one to my heart,
And I love you above all the phrases of art,
For no language could frame and no lips could repeat
My rhyme-haunted raptures of Lockerbie street.

"Lovely job, Sarah," said Mrs. Woodruff, standing at the front of the bus, looking like a peacock. "And as you can see, not much has changed on this dear little street in the last hundred years."

The Fourth Grade Poetry Club disembarked the bus and gathered on the sidewalk in front of the museum. In the distance, to the left, George could see the skyscrapers of Downtown Indianapolis. The Chase Tower was the tallest. To George, it looked like a giant robot with two monstrous antennas piercing the clouds. And the line of dark windows at the top looked like the robot's eyes.

"What is that?" asked a boy named Clark Temple. He was pointing at a large block of stone at the edge of the curb.

"That is a carriage stone," Sarah quickly chimed. "It was used to step up onto a carriage or buggy."

George could see the pleased look cross Sarah's face as if she had just answered the Final Jeopardy question correctly.

"That's right," said Mrs. Woodruff.

"When's lunch?" interrupted Jake Bolton.

Sarah's look quickly changed from "pleased" to "annoyed". Jake was the tallest kid in the whole school, even taller than the eighth graders in the middle school portion of the building.

"We'll eat after the tour," said Mrs. Woodruff. "Now, follow me up the steps to the front door. Ms. Hatfield is expecting us."

George looked up at the stately home. It was two stories high and made of red brick. The windows were tall and arched, and he could see the fancy white lace curtains on the inside. The wooden front door was also very elegant and tall, yet the doorknob was very low. George thought that was strange.

Jake was at the front of the line, so Mrs. Woodruff asked him to ring the bell, which sounded more like a buzzer than the typical "ding-dong".

They waited for a little over a minute, but nobody answered. Mrs. Woodruff pushed her way to the front and rang the bell again and again.

No answer.

Finally, George heard footsteps quickly approaching the door. Quite clumsily the door swung open, and a nicely dressed lady in a white blazer with purple polka dots and a long skirt welcomed them in.

"I'm so sorry about that," she said as she waved everyone into the dark front hallway. "I was in the middle of something."

George noticed two things about the lady immediately. She spoke in a heavy Southern drawl, and her hair was flattened to one side as if she had fallen down or something. She must have noticed his glance because she immediately patted her hair-do back into place.

"Welcome to the James Whitcomb Riley Museum Home," she drawled. "My name is Judy Hatfield. I'm the museum historian, preservationist and your tour guide."

Just then a loud BANG came from underneath the floor.

"Good heavens," Mrs. Woodruff shrieked. "What on Earth was that?"

"Excuse me," said Ms. Hatfield as she hurried down the dark hallway and disappeared around the corner.

George could hear a door creak open followed by some strange gurgling noises. When Ms. Hatfield returned he could have sworn he smelled pickles.

"James Whitcomb Riley was born in Greenfield, Indiana on October 7, 1849." Ms. Hatfield jumped into her spiel as if nothing had happened. "He was known as the Hoosier Poet, but many referred to him as the Children's Poet, since he wrote many of his poems for children, like you. He lived in this house for the last quarter century of his life as an honored guest of the Nickum and Holstein families. In fact, they considered him a family member."

"You've given this tour thousands of times, haven't you?" said Sarah. "By the cadence of your voice, I can tell that your speech is memorized."

George could tell by Ms. Hatfield's nervous laugh that she was caught off-guard by Sarah's observation.

"After seventeen years of working here," said Ms. Hatfield, "I suppose I could give this tour in my sleep, but I take my job here seriously."

Just before Sarah opened her mouth to continue her assessment, Mrs. Woodruff placed a firm hand on her shoulder. "That's quite enough, Sarah." she said. "Thank you."

Ms. Hatfield showed them the drawing room where Mr. Riley's player piano still stood near a wall. She showed them the library, which they learned was Mr. Riley's favorite room. Volumes of his personal book collection filled the shelves. And before they went upstairs, they were shown the formal dining room with the fancy china and silver displayed as if a dinner party would begin at any moment.

"Now, if you look up the staircase, you will see a rose-colored window at the landing," said Ms. Hatfield. "Would anyone like to guess what that window was for?"

Of course, Sarah's hand shot straight up before anyone else's.

"Okay, young lady," said Ms. Hatfield. "Go ahead."

"Victorians loved their stained glass windows, and this window is obviously rose colored to complement the red carpet of the staircase."

"No, but good guess," said Ms. Hatfield, showing some obvious pleasure in Sarah's wrong answer.

George raised his hand.

"Yes, young man."

"Was it a secret window? I mean - the kind that you can see out of, but people on the other side can't see in?"

"You are the first person to guess that correctly," said Ms. Hatfield, grinning.

George could feel Sarah's laser eyes burning a hole through the back of his head.

Upstairs, Ms. Hatfield showed the poetry club the bedrooms of John and Charlotte Nickum on the right side of the hallway, and their daughter and son-in-law's master bedroom on the left. Their names were Charles and Magdalena Holstein.

Then she directed them to Mr. Riley's bedroom.

"This is the best room in the house," said Ms. Hatfield. "If you look on Mr. Riley's bed, you will see his top hat and cane, and right next to that is a little poodle named Lockerbie. She guards the Poet's room."

Ms. Hatfield looked directly at George and winked.

"Guards the room from what?" asked Jake. "Who'd want to steal this crap?"

"Jake!" said Mrs. Woodruff through her teeth. "That was rude."

"All the items in Mr. Riley's bedroom were his personal belongings," insisted Ms. Hatfield. "They're each a special piece of Indiana history and would be impossible to replace."

"The James Whitcomb Riley Museum is the only true Victorian preservation in the country," chimed Sarah. "Most museums are full of replicas or replacements of period antiques."

"You've done your homework," said Ms. Hatfield.

"I always do," replied Sarah, crossing her arms and shifting her weight to one hip.

Ms. Hatfield slipped back into her spiel without giving Sarah's last comment any attention.

"If you look above the fireplace, you will see a painting of Lockerbie as well," continued Ms. Hatfield. "She was a gift to Mr. Riley from Mrs. Holstein. Lockerbie followed Mr. Riley everywhere he went. They were inseparable."

"Is that the desk where Mr. Riley wrote his poetry?" asked Mrs. Woodruff, pointing to a fancy wooden desk across the room. "The chair looks so tiny."

"Yes, Mr. Riley used that desk to write some of his later poetry," answered Ms. Hatfield. "As for the chair, Mr. Riley, like most Victorian people, was much smaller than people are today. Have you noticed how low the doorknobs are and how short the beds were made?"

"Must be all the chemicals they add to our food," said Jeremy Fletcher, who usually never said anything. "My mom is a scientist Downtown. She told me all about it."

"Could be," said Ms. Hatfield with a chuckle as she ushered the group further down the hall.

George stayed behind and took a closer look at Mr. Riley's bedroom. The hat and cane looked exactly like those belonging to the man in the audience. He glanced at the stuffed poodle with the little pink ribbon on her head. He could've sworn that she was closer to the center of the bed the last time he had looked. Now, she was closer to the edge.

"George!" Mrs. Woodruff whispered sternly. "Keep up."

Ms. Hatfield showed the students the first bathroom in Indianapolis to have running water. Considering that people were smaller during those days, George noticed that the toilet was huge, almost like a throne. He caught himself laughing out loud but stopped before anyone really noticed.

"The next room is Katie Kendall's bedroom," Ms. Hatfield continued. "She was the home's housekeeper and had the only bedroom without a fireplace, but she did have a vent in the floor that received heat from the kitchen stove below. Ms. Kendall's room was probably the warmest in the house, since the stove was almost always in use."

At the end of the long hallway there was a narrow flight of stairs.

"Now, watch your head as you go down to the kitchen," said Ms. Hatfield. "And when you get there, gather in the middle by the sink."

Most of the other rooms were kind of dark and restful, but the kitchen had windows on almost every wall. It was certainly the brightest room in the house.

"Probably the most interesting feature of the Riley Home is the old intercom system," said Ms. Hatfield. "Do you see that box on the wall with the little knobs that go up and down? And do you see the tube beneath it? Each room upstairs has a tube just like it. When someone needed service, they would blow into the tube and the corresponding knob would rise to indicate what room Ms. Kendall or Mr. Ewing the butler would attend to."

George's attention perked at hearing the butler's last name.

"Did you say, Ewing?" he blurted. "Because that's my last name!"

"Maybe you are related to Dennis, the Butler."

"Wait. Dennis is my dad's name! People call him Denny."

"Probably just a coincidence," said Mrs. Woodruff. "I'm sure there are tons of Ewing's in a city this big."

George didn't brush it off that quickly. "Was the butler

black?"

"Yes, he was," said Ms. Hatfield. "He and his wife, Nannie Ewing, actually lived in a small apartment above the carriage house."

"Ewing is a very common African American name." Sarah inserted that bit of knowledge as if she were some kind of gate keeper of American genealogical records.

"How would you know?" said Brittany Beville. George could tell that she had been waiting to knock Sarah down a peg or two.

"We'll figure that out later," said Mrs. Woodruff. "Let Ms. Hatfield finish our tour."

Ms. Hatfield gave George an approving smile – a smile that told him that she thought there was a special link, too. But she went on with the tour, anyway.

"Now, imagine that Mr. Riley is up late one night writing a poem, and he gets hungry for a snickerdoodle cookie, his favorite," said Ms. Hatfield. "All he would have to do is blow…"

"My grandma makes snickerdoodles," George shouted. "Just yesterday…"

"Everybody's grandma makes snickerdoodles," Sarah butted in.

"Not mine," said Brittany, shaking her head, then fixing her gaze at the corner of the room.

"That's quite e-nough!" snapped Mrs. Woodruff.

Ms. Hatfield smiled and opened her mouth to continue the kitchen tour when another loud BANG came from under the floor.

"I'm terribly sorry," she said. "I'm going to have to end the tour here. You see… I have… Well, there is a problem in the basement. You can show yourselves out the back door. Just follow the sidewalk to the front."

And with that, she disappeared around another corner.

And as Mrs. Woodruff led the poetry club out the back door, George smelled the pickles again.

Chapter 4

When George got home from school, he found Granny in the kitchen peeling potatoes. She wore her Saturday housecoat – the green one with purple and orange flowers all over it. As a matter of fact, all of her housecoats had flowers on them.

"Who is Dad named after?" he asked.

"His grandfather, just like you're named after your grandfather. It's a Ewing tradition," said Granny. "The names alternate, Dennis to George and so forth. I thought you already..."

"I did," said George.

"What's come over you, child? What kind of life or death riddle are you trying to solve?"

"Why do you make snickerdoodles?" said George, sitting down across the table from Granny.

She wrinkled her face. "Because you and your dad like them. What kind of question is that?"

"So you just found a recipe one day and decided to try it out?"

"No, it's in the Book."

That was all George needed to hear. Granny was in charge of the Book – a family heirloom that had been passed down from generation to generation. It was full of family recipes and history, and it was simply known as "the Book".

"This is too weird," said George, resting his head in his hands.

"What is wrong with you, boy? Why are you acting like this?"

"James Whitcomb Riley's butler was named Dennis Ewing!"

"Oh," said Granny. "Was he black?"

"Yes, and Mr. Riley's favorite cookies were snickerdoodles!"

"What was the butler's wife's name?" asked Granny.

"I think Ms. Hatfield said it was Nannie or..."

"She wrote the first recipes in the Book," said Granny. "Her name is on the inside cover."

"It's true then," said George.

"Peel these potatoes," said Granny, "while I get the Book. We've got family records all the way back to the Civil War."

George didn't peel a single potato while he waited for Granny to return. His mind was fixed on Mr. Riley's butler. There was no way it was a coincidence. The name wasn't John Smith or Bob Johnson. It was Dennis Ewing. How many people with that name could have lived in Indianapolis in the late 1800's with a wife named Nannie? George's hypothesis was... ONE!

"Here it is," said Granny, returning to the kitchen. She wiped her hand across the old book and opened the front cover. She also placed a large chunk of purple crystal on the table. "Amethyst! For protection, especially if ghosts are following you around."

George began to put the crystal in his right pocket.

"Left pocket," said Granny.

George wanted to ask why it mattered, but he was more interested in the names in the book. He remembered Granny using the Book many times, but he had never gone through the pages himself. First of all, it was homemade and looked kind of fragile. The paper was brown and the cover was frayed and battered.

Granny pulled her half-moon, bifocal glasses from her housecoat pocket and turned to a page towards the back. She ran her finger down the list of faded names. "There," she said, sliding the book in front of George.

"Dennis Ewing. Born 1860. Moved to Indianapolis from Tennessee in 1880," George read from the Book.

"I think you found the butler," said Granny, looking at George over her glasses

"He had a wife named Nannie," said George, "and a son named George. And George had a son named Dennis... all the way up to me. Wow! I'm in the Book too."

"Of course you are," said Granny.

They were interrupted by the slamming of the front

door.

"Good news!" called Mr. Ewing, rushing into the kitchen.

"You scared the daylights out of me, son!" said Granny with her hand over her heart. "Don't you know better than to barge in on an old lady like that?"

Mr. Ewing paid his mother no attention. "You are looking at the new Master Groundskeeper of Crown Hill Cemetery!"

Granny gasped, moving her hand from her heart to her mouth.

"I leave for a special training at Arlington National Cemetery tomorrow morning," Mr. Ewing continued. "I'll be training with master groundskeepers from cemeteries all over the world!"

"That's awesome, Dad!"

"Denny, I am so proud of you," said Granny. "Hard work pays off. Thank you, Lord!"

George's dad had worked at Crown Hill since he was in high school. He had started working only in the summers, and when he graduated, they hired him full time.

"George, you'll have to hold down the fort while I'm gone," he said. "Do what Granny says."

That was a given. He had learned that one a long time ago.

"Let's celebrate!" said Granny, opening a small canister on the kitchen table. She pulled out two dollars. "George, run down to the gas station and buy some root beer. I'll make floats after dinner."

George took the two dollars and ran out the door. He loved root beer floats just as much as snickerdoodles, and having them both in the same week was a rare treat.

On his way to the gas station, George looked across the street into the cemetery. He hoped he might catch another glimpse of Mr. Riley's ghost, but no such luck. In fact, a storm cloud loomed over the eastern sky, so George knew he had better hurry to make it back before the rain.

George rushed inside the gas station and grabbed Granny's favorite root beer, A&W. He quickly paid the clerk and dashed towards home. He could smell the rain, and he noticed the leaves on the silver maples turning towards the sky, waiting for the downpour. The wind picked up and carried some dust and litter across the street.

As George quickened his pace, he saw a little white dog out of the corner of his eye. Just as he turned his head for a better look, it disappeared. He looked straight ahead, and again, he saw the little white dog. This time he snapped his head towards that direction, but the dog disappeared.

Just as George leapt to the top of the front porch steps, great sheets of rain poured from the sky. He looked back to see if the little dog was there, but he saw nothing.

"Get in here," said his Dad. "You'll get struck by lightning!"

"I should've never sent you out there," said Granny. "I had no idea a storm was workin' up like that."

George really didn't pay his family much attention. His eyes were still glued to the other side of the street as his dad hustled him inside. The scent of grass clippings and gasoline was still on his dad's clothes.

"Poor dog," George mumbled. "I hope he's okay."

Chapter 5

George and his family celebrated his dad's promotion with Granny's Chicken N' Dumplings over mashed potatoes. Unlike the snickerdoodle recipe that had come from Grandpa George's side of the family, Granny's dumplings was hers alone. And they were good!

After the storm had settled, they sat on the back porch, enjoying their root beer floats and watching the lightning bugs blink on and off in the darkness.

"These are the days I wish your Momma was here, George," said his dad. "She'd be proud of both of us today.

You just finished the fourth grade, and I got a promotion."

When his mom was alive, they had an apartment on the other side of the cemetery, but after she died, George and his father had a hard time living there. Everything reminded them of her, from paint colors on the walls to the coffee stain on the carpet. They began spending nights with Granny. One night turned into to two and two turned into to three and so on. That's when Granny decided that it would be best for everyone if they just moved in.

"She loved you very much," said Mr. Ewing. "She loved reading to you, too."

"I remember," said George, spooning the last of the ice cream from the bottom of his mug. "Curious George books were my favorite."

"Mine too," said Mr. Ewing. "The set you have belonged to me when I was a boy."

"Sure did," Granny remembered. "Your dad bought them for you. He thought it was funny that a monkey carried his name."

Mr. Ewing laughed. "A little monkey named George," he said.

George noticed Granny's eyes getting a little wet.

"So much love in our little house tonight," she said. "I sure wish they were here."

"What happened to Grandpa George?"

Granny got up from her big cushioned chair and headed inside. "Go ahead and tell him, Denny. He's old enough to know."

George's dad took a deep breath and began a story that had shaken their family to the core.

"You see, son, there's a reason why Granny never leaves the house," his dad began. "A long time ago, Grandpa George worked at Beveridge Paper Company on White River."

"Close to where we go fishing at Riverside Park?" George interrupted.

"Further downtown, closer to the zoo," said Mr. Ewing. "It's torn down now, but Grandpa George was killed in a car accident on his way there one morning."

"Wow," said George. "I bet you were sad."

"I was very sad, and so was Granny," Mr. Ewing added.

"How old were you?" asked George.

"Your age," said Mr. Ewing. "It was the summer before fifth grade."

George thought about that for a moment. He knew what it was like to lose his mother at the age of five, but he didn't even want to imagine what it would be like to lose his dad at ten.

"The day after the funeral, Granny drove herself to the flower shop just down the road. She wanted to pay her bill," Mr. Ewing continued. "But she was robbed in the parking lot. The man stole the diamond ring Grandpa George gave her on their wedding day."

"What?!" said George. He put his empty mug on the porch floor and leaned closer to his dad.

"Granny drove home and didn't leave the house again until the following Easter Sunday," said Mr. Ewing. "She said that the world had taken enough from her. Over twenty years later, she feels the same."

Just then, the screen door opened, and Granny joined them again. As she sat back down in her big cushioned chair, George noticed that she had something in her hand. It looked like a dried flower.

"What is that, Momma?" asked Mr. Ewing.

"A rose from your dad's casket," said Granny, her eyes glistening. "I've kept it inside my jewelry box since that day."

"I didn't know you had that?" said Mr. Ewing, pulling

his billfold from his back pocket. He moved the money to one side and slid out a small envelope.

"What's in there?" asked George.

Mr. Ewing opened the envelope and three petals fell out. "Rose petals," he said. "From your mom's funeral. One for her, one for me, and one for you."

"Ain't that something," said Granny. "You certainly are my son."

Mr. Ewing put his arm around George and squeezed him tight. "Grampa George and your Mom were very special people. We miss them, but what's amazing is that you have both of them living inside of you."

"They live right here," said Granny, patting George on his chest. "And that's what makes our world right."

"But the world isn't right if you can't leave the house, Granny?"

"There ain't nothin' out there for me, honey," she said. "Everything I need is right here, you see?"

George didn't pry any further. And when Granny grabbed and held his hand, he knew that her troubles were deeper than he could understand. So, they all sat back and continued watching the lightning bugs.

Upstairs, George tossed and turned in his bed. His lights were off but his room wasn't dark. The clouds were gone and bright light from the moon shone through his window.

He thought about his family and all the tragedy that they had been through. In his very short life, he had experienced a lot, but now he understood why he and his dad had moved in with Granny. He also realized that loss could bring a family closer together. And his house was certainly full of love.

As George's eyelids grew heavier and heavier, he thought more about his mom. Her name was Wendy just like the girl in his favorite book, *Peter Pan.* And somewhere like Neverland, he knew his mother was waiting for him and his dad. Grandpa George was there too, waiting to hold Granny's hand.

With peaceful thoughts on his mind, George drifted off to sleep but was quickly woken up by a barking dog.

Chapter 6:

George jerked his legs toward his chest and backed himself up against the headboard.

"I'm a girl, not a boy," said a sophisticated voice at the foot of George's bed. "And I'm sorry if I have frightened you, but we need your help."

Still terrified, George responded, "Who are you, and uh, where are you?"

Just then, a small white poodle jumped up onto the bed. "I hope you don't mind a canine on your bedding," said the poodle. "It's simply what I've grown accustomed to."

George's mouth dropped. "Lockerbie?" he said slowly.

"The Ghost of Lockerbie, to be precise," said the poodle.

George noticed the dog's soft glow and transparency.

"I saw you earlier on the street, didn't I?" asked George.

"Precisely," said Lockerbie. "And you called me a 'he', and as you can see, I am perfectly a 'she'."

With that, Lockerbie jumped up onto George's knees and stared directly into his face. "I knew immediately that you were a descendant of Ewing, the Butler."

"How?" said George, his eyes widening.

"I never forget a scent," said Lockerbie. "And you smell just like him."

"That's weird."

"Not really," insisted Lockerbie. "But anyway, we've been looking for you."

"Why?" said George, beginning to feel a bit creeped out.

"Unfinished business," said Lockerbie. "Ewing, the Butler began something that you, my friend, must finish."

"Does it have something to do with Mr. Riley's ghost?" said George. "I saw him the other day."

"Well, he doesn't just let anybody see his spirit," said Lockerbie. "For the last ninety-nine years, it has only been me."

George looked more intently at the canine ghost before him. She was pearly white and translucent just like any ghost should be.

"Does he want me to do something?" he said.

"I don't have all the answers yet," said Lockerbie. "But we can start by retrieving the humidor. The goblins broke through the basement door and stole it."

"That's what that noise was beneath the floor!"

"Precisely," said Lockerbie. "The Goblin Hole is down there. Judy has done her best over the years to keep them from intruding, but they are persistent creatures, to say the least."

"But what is a humidor?"

"Mr. Riley's cigar box," Lockerbie elaborated. "It holds the Squidgicum Squee, but the spell is winding down, and the Goblin King apparently knows this! He'll release the Squidgicum Squee from the humidor, and then all of Mr. Riley's poetry will be erased from history."

"Squidgicum Squee," said George. "I recognize that from one of the Riley poems."

"The Raggedy Man," said Lockerbie.

"That's right. Doesn't it swallow itself or something?"

"Think of it as a giant eraser," said Lockerbie. "It erases whatever it swallows, and the Goblin King possessed it for many years before it was trapped in the humidor."

"But what's the big deal? Why does the Goblin King want it?"

"Books!" said Lockerbie. "Books are special, and when the Squidgicum Squee swallows a book, it regurgitates it into a puff of silver or gold. The goblins collect the gold and melt it into coins."

"What about the silver?"

"They aren't interested in silver. That's why they only feed the Squidgicum Squee books written for children. Only those books produce the gold. The rest make silver."

"Interesting," said George. "But what do goblins do with these gold coins?"

"They hoard them," explained Lockerbie. "Goblins love gold more than anything - more than each other, I've been told. And they could care less that the books they throw to the Squidgicum Squee are erased from history, FOREVER!"

"But there are sometimes thousands of copies of the same book. The goblins can't get them all, can they?"

"It only takes one copy to erase ALL of the others. And I'm sure the goblins have hoards of books, including Mr. Riley's, just waiting to be erased forever all in the name of gold."

George scooted to the side of his bed. "This is a lot for me to take in," he said. "First of all, I'm talking to a dog."

"A poodle."

"Okay, a poodle – a GHOST poodle at that," George emphasized. "And this ghost poodle wants me to believe that goblins are feeding children's books to a mythical creature so that it will barf up gold. And you want me to stop it!"

"That sums it up, although I'd omit the word 'barf,'" said Lockerbie. "What a precisely foul word."

"Vomit," said George. "Is that better?"

Lockerbie jumped back onto the bed. "So, will you assist me?"

"Sure," said George. "But I can't come with you tonight. If Granny finds me missing, she will flip out."

"Tomorrow, then," said Lockerbie. "Judy and I should be fine until then. I'll be waiting for you at the southwest corner of the cemetery in the morning - nine o'clock!"

"Who's Judy?"

"Ms. Hatfield, silly."

And with that, she vanished.

Chapter 7

The savory smell of sausage frying in a hot iron skillet enticed George from his slumber. Granny didn't usually make breakfast. Toast and eggs was about as far as she'd go, but he remembered that his Dad was headed to Washington D.C. that morning, which made it a special occasion.

George got up and took a quick shower, and as he got dressed he replayed his conversation with Lockerbie. He wondered if maybe it had all been a dream, but he quickly disregarded that idea and started planning how he'd get out of the house. He was supposed to meet Lockerbie at the southwest corner of Crown Hill by 9:00am.

Over breakfast, George wanted to tell his family about the Goblin Hole and the Squidgicum Squee, but he knew he should keep it to himself. The ghost business had surely been enough for one week.

"Anymore fieldtrips?" asked Granny. She was in her Sunday housecoat. It was black with sparkling, gold lilies all over it.

"Nope," said George, chomping down a sausage link. "But can I go over to the cemetery later to do some research?"

"On what?" asked Mr. Ewing. "You know I won't be over there to keep an eye on you."

"I'm in fifth grade, dad," he said.

"Well, you check in with Granny on the hour," insisted Mr. Ewing.

Just then, a car horn honked.

"Must be the cab," said Mr. Ewing, standing up from the table and wiping his mouth with a napkin. "Wish me luck!"

"Call me as soon as you get to the hotel," said Granny.

"Good luck, Dad!"

Mr. Ewing rushed toward the front door where his luggage was waiting. George and Granny followed him and stood on the porch while the cab driver loaded everything in the trunk. And as the cab drove away, George watched his dad wave from the back window.

"He's movin' up in the world," said Granny, waving back.

"He's the boss!" said George, waving too.

"On that side of the fence, he is," she said, pointing toward the cemetery. "On this side, it's a different story. There's only one boss in this house."

George snickered and bumped his grandmother with his elbow. "That's right," he said. "Me."

"Child, you've lost your mind!"

If losing one's mind included conversations with phantom poodles, then George could certainly check that box.

Back inside, George finished his breakfast, while Granny washed the dishes and sang. He couldn't remember a time that Granny didn't sing while scrubbing pots and pans. By now, he recognized almost all of the songs. This time is was *Someday We'll be Together* by Diana Ross and the Supremes. She sang this song more than any other, and now, George understood why. It was a song about two people kept far apart but knowing that someday they'd be together again. Granny was singing to Grandpa George.

Taking his empty plate to the sink and slipping it into the dish water, George grabbed a towel and starting drying the rinsed dishes. He didn't know all of the words to Granny's song, but he hummed along with her.

When they were through, he went upstairs to pack his backpack. He had no idea what one should take down the Goblin Hole, but he decided that a flashlight would be a wise choice. He also threw in a few books and a notepad.

That's when he realized that he should probably write Granny a note. He would write the whole truth and explain to her why he hadn't told her in person. He couldn't risk her refusing to let him go.

George wrote the letter, folded it up and stuffed it inside his back pocket.

Chapter 8

George grabbed his baseball cap from the coat stand by the door. It was red with his first initial embroidered in blue. His mom had given it to him for Christmas the year she died. Now, George went nowhere without it. Luckily, it was a snapback cap with size adjustments.

He stuffed the letter in the mailbox and bolted down the steps to the sidewalk. The sun was hot, and the air was humid from the storm the night before. It was a good thing he had put on shorts and a t-shirt, although he was already sweating beneath his backpack. Disregarding the heat, he jogged towards the southwest corner of the cemetery.

"I was hoping you hadn't lost your nerve," said Lockerbie as George turned the corner.

George looked around and saw Lockerbie sitting on a rock between two spruce trees. He squeezed through a wide hole in the fencing and walked over to her.

"Reporting for duty!" said George, with his hand raised in a salute.

"I'm glad to see some enthusiasm," said Lockerbie. "The goblins came back last night and tied Judy to a basement pipe. They tried to interrogate her for more information."

"That's terrible!"

"And since I'm a ghost, I can't use my teeth to untie her."

"Do you think we can get all of this done before dark," asked George. "Granny is going to be worried…"

Lockerbie's eyes darted around, looking in all directions. "Take the ribbon from my head," she insisted.

"Why?" asked George.

"Trust me," said Lockerbie. "I'm one hundred and fifteen years old. I know what I'm doing."

George scratched his head, trying to do the math. "I guess you're right."

"Precisely," said Lockerbie. "I usually am."

George finally followed her instructions and was surprised that he could actually touch and feel the ribbon. The rest of Lockerbie's body was like a hologram. You could see it, but you couldn't touch it.

"Now, close your eyes and count backwards from ten."

"Is this some kind of hocus pocus?" asked George.

"We could walk the three miles if you prefer."

George closed his eyes and counted backwards. He instantly felt cold, as if he had walked into a freezer. His body tingled with goosebumps, and by the time he got to three, he tried to open his eyes, but they wouldn't budge.

"two... one..." he said.

"Open your eyes," said Lockerbie.

George recognized the room instantly. They had somehow teleported straight to Mr. Riley's bedroom.

"H-h-how did you do that?" George stuttered.

"Magic," she said with a wink.

"What else can this little ribbon do?" asked George as he ran the soft satin through his fingers.

"I'm really not sure," said Lockerbie. "I wasn't the one who charmed it."

"Who did?"

"More about that later," said Lockerbie, "but for right now, place the ribbon back on my head, please."

George followed her directions and watched the ribbon magically tie itself back into a bow. "AMAZING!" he said.

"Follow me," said Lockerbie, leaping down from Mr. Riley's bed. "We must release Judy."

George looked at Lockerbie and then back at the stuffed version of her on the bed. "When I was here the other day, did you move that stuffed poodle?"

"I got your attention, didn't I?"

"Yes, but how? I thought you couldn't touch things."

"I can only move things in Mr. Riley's room."

George nodded his head slowly. There was so much for him to comprehend.

As Lockerbie led George to the first floor, he realized that the museum was THE perfect haunted house. All of the rooms were immaculately furnished and roped off from current day people. And once Ms. Hatfield went home, George could imagine the ghosts roaming around, unbothered.

"Are you the only ghost in this house?" asked George.

"Yes, but I'm not the only spirit."

"There's a difference?"

"Ghosts are kind of stuck," explained Lockerbie as she descended the stairs. "But spirits can come and go as they please."

"Are you stuck?"

"I like to think of it as unfinished business," Lockerbie insisted.

"What about Mr. Riley?" George asked as he followed Lockerbie around the corner to the basement door.

"Spirit," said Lockerbie. "He comes and goes as he pleases, but I'm the only one who can see him, until recently, I suppose."

Just then George heard a faint cry for help.

"That's Judy," said Lockerbie. "She must know we're here."

Lockerbie walked through the door just like a ghost would, but George had to use the doorknob. By the time George opened the door, Lockerbie was already at the foot of the basement stairs. "Hurry," she said.

The basement was cold and damp, but George could smell a soft scent of perfume. He followed Lockerbie into a narrow room with shelves on each side. These shelves were packed with seasonal decorations, and hanging between them was a lightbulb.

"I was afraid you had forgotten about me," said Ms. Hatfield in her Southern drawl. She was wrapped in ropes and tied to a pipe that ran down the wall.

George immediately got to work, untying the ropes. As he pulled at the knots, he saw a gigantic spider scurry towards the shadowy corner. He kept that tidbit of information to himself.

"Well, young Mr. Ewing, I'm happy to see you," said Ms. Hatfield. "I knew Lockerbie would find you. Quite the little sniffer, she's got."

"Thank you, Ms. Hatfield," said George as he untied the last knot. "I think you're free."

"Please call me, Judy," she said as George helped her to her feet. He could see that she was wearing the same clothes that she had on the day of the tour – the polka dotted blazer and long skirt.

"Did you see it?" asked Judy as she stretched her arms. "You stepped right over it."

George looked behind himself and saw a soft yellow glow coming from a perfectly round hole in the ground. A perfectly cold chill ran right up his spine, too.

"Should we close it?" he asked frantically, noticing the lid by its side.

"They aren't coming back," said Judy. "They have the humidor with the Squidgicum Squee locked inside."

"But we must take it back," said Lockerbie, stamping her front paws.

George peered into the hole. He had imagined that it would resemble a sewer, but it was quite clean. The hole led to what looked like a perfect stone tunnel, but it smelled like… pickles. Judy must have noticed him sniffing.

"Goblins eat anything that's pickled," she said. "I've thrown at least six thousand pickles down that hole to keep those little monsters out of the house."

"Where did you get that many pickles?" asked Geroge.

"Directly from the pickle factory!" said Judy. "I spent a whole month's salary on gherkins."

"All thrown down the tube, so to speak," said Lockerbie, at the edge of the Goblin Hole.

"Looks like we'll be going down the tube, too," said George.

"Precisely," said Lockerbie. "It's been a hundred years since I've been down there. I hope I still know my way around."

At that moment the floorboards creaked above them.
"Did you hear that?" said George.

Chapter 9

All three of them slowly walked up the basement steps. George could hear what sounded like keys jangling on a keyring.

"The library," said Judy. "Somebody's in the library."

Lockerbie zoomed ahead and vanished through the wall. In a split second, she returned. "You've got to see this!"

They followed her to the library where a little green goblin was busy trying to break into one of the locked bookcases.

"That little weasel has my master keyring!" shouted

Judy. She threw back the guard rope and charged at the goblin. "Hand them over, right now!"

George didn't realize that goblins were so small and so finely dressed. This little guy was a mere two feet tall and wore a red and yellow checkered suit that reminded George of ketchup and mustard. The creature turned around and gave Judy a toothy smile.

"Should she be that close to a goblin?" George asked Lockerbie.

"If there is anyone who can handle goblins, it's Judy," insisted Lockerbie. "She's had many run-ins with the little devils."

"Books," said the Goblin. "Spurlock must read all the books."

The goblin turned back around and continued trying each key in the lock.

"Those books don't belong to you," snapped Judy, pulling a pickle from her pocket. "But this does."

"Pickled cucumbers!" the goblin squealed. "Spurlock loves pickled cucumbers."

George couldn't believe his eyes. Judy was reasoning with a goblin.

"Spurlock wants books more than pickled cucumbers!" he stated and turned back to the cabinet.

George remembered that he was still carrying his backpack. He released a strap from one of his arms and unzipped the largest compartment. Inside was his favorite copy of Peter Pan. "Boy, do I have a great book for you," he said. "The pages are full of pirates and fairies…"

The Goblin turned to face him, and George could see that he was reading the cover. Just then, the little green man doubled over in laughter. "Peter's in the Pan!" He laughed. "Well, he better get out or he'll burn his bum!"

George scrunched his eyebrows. "It's not Peter in the

Pan, silly." But the goblin paid no attention to this. He dropped the keys and hobbled over to George. Lockerbie growled, which sent the goblin hobbling back to the other side of the room. Judy quickly snatched the keys and put them in her pocket.

"He's afraid of you," George said to Lockerbie.

"He smells familiar," Lockerbie said between growls.

"Let's make a deal," said George. "Your name is Spurlock, right?"

"Spurlock's the name, keeper of books is my game!" said the goblin, taking a seat on a fancy Victorian footstool. He crossed his legs and rested his knobby little hands in his lap. George got a good look at his eyes. They were green with sparkling gold flecks.

"Don't let him charm you," said Lockerbie, still growling. "And whatever you do, don't give him that book. It will be swallowed by the Squidgicum Squee and erased from history."

"Lockerbie is right," said Judy. "He'll take it to the Goblin King."

"Goblin King!" Spurlock spat. "Spurlock hates the Goblin King!"

"George looked at Judy and then down at Lockerbie. They both gave him the same look – one of utter bewilderment.

"You don't work for the Goblin King?" asked George.

Spurlock appeared to be gagging himself on his own saliva. "I'd rather swallow a billy goat WHOLE than work for that tyrant!"

"But don't you want gold?" George said, trying to keep the information flowing.

"Spurlock has enough gold," he sputtered. "Spurlock needs books."

An idea popped into George's head. "And the Goblin

King is trying to steal your books!" If the idea hadn't already been planted in Spurlock's head, it was now.

Spurlock stomped his little feet. The gold buckles on his shoes glimmered each time a foot hit the floor. "Spurlock hates the Goblin King! Spurlock wants to chop off his head."

Even Judy stepped back with that comment. "Oh, my," she said.

"Well, we want to find the Goblin King. He took something from us too." insisted George. "Do you know about the Squidgicum Squee?"

"Spurlock despises the Squee! The Squee will swallow Spurlock's books when the Century Spell is broken."

It was making more and more sense to George. The Goblin King was using Spurlock's addiction for hoarding books to his advantage. Spurlock would steal the books, and the Goblin King would take them. There is probably a great hoard of books cached away for when the spell is broken on the humidor.

George pulled out two more books from his backpack. "If you help us find the Goblin King, I will give you all three of these books."

"Spurlock likes the deal you've offered, but Spurlock wants Peter in the Pan now."

George could see the apprehension in Judy's face, and a low growl escaped Lockerbie's mouth. But George trusted his own intuition and knew that he was on the right track. He tossed his copy of *Peter Pan* to Spurlock. They were all surprised when Spurlock clutched the book to his chest and sat down on the floor.

"Spurlock is in for a treat, something that pickles and gold could never beat," said the Goblin, opening the book to the first page.

George was pleased that the goblin didn't try running

for the basement and towards the Goblin Hole. Maybe his plan was going to work, but he needed to know more about the spell on the humidor.

George looked down at Lockerbie. "Do you know anything else about this century spell?"

Lockerbie took a deep breath and exhaled slowly. "I was there when the spell was made." said Lockerbie. "And Ewing, the Butler told us that it would last only a hundred years after Mr. Riley's death."

"That's less than a month away," said Judy. "Mr. Riley died on July 22, 1916."

"How would Ewing, the Butler know this much about the spell?" asked George.

Lockerbie sat on her haunches and looked into George's eyes. "Because he made it."

Chapter 10

Spurlock hadn't moved an inch from his spot on the library floor. George and Judy had sat down in the cathedral chairs in the front hallway, while Lockerbie guarded the library door next to them.

"See that painting right there," said Judy. "Richard Gruelle painted it. There are cows in that field, but you can only see them on a bright sunny day when the light comes through the windows just right."

George only half-heard what Judy was saying. His mind was occupied with what he had just learned about his fifth great-grandfather. Things were starting to make some sense. Granny did all kinds of strange little hocus-pocus things around the house - just like the moonstone she had given to him to calm his nerves. He wondered if that was some kind of spell.

"His son was Johnny Gruelle," said Judy. "Are you familiar with him?"

George's attention turned back to Judy. "I don't think so," he said.

"Ever heard of Raggedy Ann and Andy?"

Those names did sound familiar to George, but he couldn't remember why.

Judy pointed to a pin she wore on her lapel. "Right here," she said. "This is Raggedy Ann. She's a ragdoll."

"Granny has a doll like that," said George, remembering the little red-yarn-haired doll between the pillows on Granny's bed.

"Well," said Judy. "Johnny Gruelle took two of Mr. Riley's poems, put them together and created new stories about Raggedy Ann and Raggedy Andy. He painted beautiful illustrations of them too, and the dolls and books were eventually sold all over the world."

"Let me guess," said George. "Little Orphant Annie and the Raggedy Man were the poems."

"That's right," said Judy. "Mr. Riley was friends with Johnny's father, and they would visit this house all of the time. I like to think of Mr. Riley as Raggedy Ann and Andy's grandpa."

Judy stood up and walked toward the dining room. "I'll be right back."

George's thoughts immediately returned back to the spell that Ewing, the Butler had made for Mr. Riley. He wondered if Granny or his dad had any idea that there was that kind of magic in their family tree.

"Here you go," said Judy, pulling George back from his thoughts. She handed him one of the yarn-haired dolls.

"Raggedy Andy!" said Lockerbie. "Ain't he an awful good raggedy boy?"

With that, Lockerbie recited the whole poem.

O the Raggedy Man! He works fer Pa;
An' he's the goodest man ever you saw!
He comes to our house every day,
An' waters the horses, an' feeds 'em hay;
An' he opens the shed—an' we all ist laugh
When he drives out our little old wobble-ly calf;
An' nen—ef our hired girl says he can—
He milks the cow fer 'Lizabuth Ann.—
Ain't he a' awful good Raggedy Man?
Raggedy! Raggedy! Raggedy Man!

W'y, The Raggedy Man—he's ist so good,
He splits the kindlin' an' chops the wood;
An' nen he spades in our garden, too,
An' does most things 'at boys can't do.—
He clumbed clean up in our big tree
An' shooked a' apple down fer me—
An' 'nother 'n', too, fer 'Lizabuth Ann—
An' 'nother 'n', too, fer The Raggedy Man.—
Ain't he a' awful kind Raggedy Man?
Raggedy! Raggedy! Raggedy Man!

An' The Raggedy Man, he knows most rhymes,
An' tells 'em, ef I be good, sometimes:
Knows 'bout Giunts, an' Griffuns, an' Elves,
An' the Squidgicum-Squees 'at swallers the'rselves:
An', wite by the pump in our pasture-lot,
He showed me the hole 'at the Wunks is got,

'At lives 'way deep in the ground, an' can
Turn into me, er 'Lizabuth Ann!
Er Ma, er Pa, er The Raggedy Man!
Ain't he a funny old Raggedy Man?
Raggedy! Raggedy! Raggedy Man!

The Raggedy Man—one time, when he
Wuz makin' a little bow-'n'-orry fer me,
Says "When you're big like your Pa is,
Air you go' to keep a fine store like his—
An' be a rich merchunt—an' wear fine clothes?—
Er what air you go' to be, goodness knows?"
An' nen he laughed at 'Lizabuth Ann,
An' I says "'M go' to be a Raggedy Man!—
I'm ist go' to be a nice Raggedy Man!"
Raggedy! Raggedy! Raggedy Man!

"Wow," said George, looking at his Raggedy Andy. He was amazed at how Mr. Riley's poems inspired so many other writers and artists. He also realized that if the Squidgicum Squee swallowed Mr. Riley's work, then a chain reaction could take place. Would Raggedy Ann and Andy be gone too?

This made George think about his own memories of reading with his mom. If the Squidgicum Squee swallowed the Curious George books or those written by Dr. Seuss, would the memories of him and his mom reading them together disappear too? George quickly decided that he would NOT let that happen.

Just as George stuffed the doll into his backpack, a loud cry of excitement came from the library. "To Neverland! Third star to the right!"

George stood up and looked through the doorway to the library. Spurlock was jumping up and down and flapping his arms.

"Spurlock, fly like Tinkerbell!" he yelled.

"Oh, dear," said Lockerbie. "The goblin has gone mad."

"Bless his little goblin heart," said Judy, placing her hand over her chest.

"Well, at least we know his weakness," said George. "And while Spurlock is engrossed in Neverland, we need to come up with a plan."

"You're right," said Lockerbie. "Shall we discuss our ideas in the drawing room? I don't believe Spurlock will be going anywhere soon."

Lockerbie breezed through the wall while George and Judy took the long way around. The main hallway separated the drawing room and the library. George thought that the drawing room was the fanciest in the house. A floor to ceiling gold mirror stood against the far wall, and a marble mantled fireplace on the next. But the ceiling was the best part. Beautiful design work was delicately painted around each corner of the ceiling, and a giant crystal gasolier hung from the center.

Judy removed the rope that kept tourists from entering the room and allowed George to go in first. "Let's sit on the piano bench," she said. "The other furniture is much more delicate."

George respected Judy's love of the museum. He could tell that she really cared for its history and preservation for generations to come. This was evident in how she handled everything so cautiously – even the light switches.

When they approached the piano bench, she and George pulled it out very slowly, like they were pulling a wooden block from a Jenga tower.

"Go ahead," she said. "Sit down."

George sat down, leaving plenty of room for her. Lockerbie stood in front of them. Her pearly white and translucent body hovered just slightly off the floor.

"George and I will have to go down the Goblin Hole right away," said Lockerbie.

"And Spurlock will be our guide," said George. "If it isn't a trick, I think Spurlock is on our side."

"I think you're right," said Judy. "And I'll stay here and give tours like everything is normal."

Chapter 11

Both George and Lockerbie peered down the Goblin Hole. Spurlock had already jumped in. He seemed eager to fulfill his duties so that he could score the other two books from George's backpack.

"You're next," said Lockerbie. "And remember, if we need to escape, just grab the ribbon from my hair and count back from ten."

George nodded and slipped himself down the Goblin Hole.

"Our future depends on you," said Judy as she slid the

cover back into place.

Wow, George thought. If that wasn't a dose of pressure, he didn't know what was. But Judy was right. It was up to him and Lockerbie to take back the humidor before the spell was broken. He wished he knew some of his ancestor's magic to keep the spell from ever breaking, but he had no idea how to get that information. This took George's thoughts back to Granny. He hoped she wasn't worried about him.

George followed Spurlock down the stone tunnel. Lockerbie followed closely behind. It was cold down there, except when they would pass a fiery torchlight.

"How many goblins are down here?" he asked. "And who keeps these torches lit?

"168 Goblins and one Goblin King," said their goblin guide. "Some light torches, some repair tunnels, but Spurlock only reads books!"

"That's just in Indianapolis," added Lockerbie. "The tunnels are connected to every city. Where there's a road, goblins have built a tunnel under it."

George jerked his head around to Lockerbie, "Under every road?"

"But the Goblin King resides right here in Indianapolis," said Lockerbie. "The Crossroads of America!"

"Aren't we lucky," George scoffed.

Just then, Spurlock took a right turn onto East Street. George could see that the tunnels were labeled with old fashioned street signs.

"Where are we headed?" asked Lockerbie.

The goblin hobbled faster. "Spurlock knows the way. Hurry up!"

George jogged to keep up with him. They took another turn - this time onto Vermont Street.

"We're headed downtown, aren't we?" said Lockerbie.

Spurlock didn't reply, but his pace quickened even more. If the situation had been lighter, George would have laughed at the sight before him. Watching the goblin run was quite funny, especially in his little ketchup and mustard suit.

George's attention was quickly diverted to a group of oncoming goblins. "Hide," he said.

"Stick with Spurlock," said their goblin guide. "Hiding won't work. Nothing gets past a goblin's nose."

George could feel his heart inching up his throat. Why didn't he ask Judy for a jar of pickles? That surely would have distracted the goblins enough to get past them. It was too late now, though. The group of goblins was just feet away.

"Spurlock has company! Let us pass!"

The other goblins didn't look nearly as nice as Spurlock. They all wore little suits, but not as colorful. They were brown and exactly the same. And their faces were greenish yellow and covered in warts. Their eyes didn't have nearly as much sparkle as Spurlock's, and they smelled like dill pickles. Luckily, they passed by without a question, although George did catch one's slobbery stare.

"Why didn't they stop us?" said Lockerbie, suspiciously. "This certainly isn't the place humans or poodles traverse much."

Spurlock seemed to ignore Lockerbie's comments. He guided them around another corner, up Pennsylvania Street – or under it, rather.

"We're headed towards the library," said Lockerbie. "What a perfect place to hide a lair full of stolen books!"

"You're right," said George. "Spurlock?"

But Spurlock didn't answer. He did seem to tuck the copy of Peter Pan further under his arm, though. Their jog had turned into a run. They passed more pickle-smelling goblins, except this group was all girls in little brown dresses. George wondered why Spurlock was the only one dressed-up.

And then they stopped! Right before them was a large hole in the ground that radiated with warm light.

"Down the ladder," said their goblin guide. "Spurlock is right behind you."

George looked at Lockerbie. He didn't even have to ask the question on his mind. She spoke up for him. "And what is down that hole, precisely?"

"You want the Squee? Spurlock will take you there."

Lockerbie gave George a nod, and he slowly climbed down the ladder to a stone landing. Since Lockerbie was a ghost, she drifted down on thin air like the feather of a dove. Spurlock slid down the ladder almost effortlessly. George could tell he had plenty of experience in this network of holes and tunnels.

Before them was a spiraling staircase. Once again, Spurlock took the lead, and down the staircase they went.

The same torches that lit the tunnels also lit the staircase, but the deeper they went, the colder it got. And if George hadn't mistaken, he thought he heard the sound of rushing water. By now, he knew better than to ask Spurlock anything. The goblin jumped three steps at a time, making it quite difficult to keep up with him.

Several minutes passed, but George could hear the water getting louder and louder. Then, all of a sudden, the stairs ended and a gigantic cavern opened up to them. It took George's breath away; it was so magnificent. Giant stalactites hung tightly to the ceiling with stalagmites growing up to meet them. A waterfall rushed down one side and emptied into a canal that split the cavern in two. A stone bridge connected both sides.

That's when George saw all of the goblins working away at something inside little rooms carved into the sides of the cavern. With a closer look he noticed that they were counting coins. GOLD COINS! Stacks and stacks of them. The torch light sent glimmers off of each stack.

"This way," said their goblin guide. "Spurlock will take you to the Squee, but first hand over the books."

"We need to see the humidor," said Lockerbie.

"No humidor, no books!" agreed George.

Spurlock's demeanor instantly changed, and before George even realized it, he and Lockerbie were surrounded by the intense smell of dill pickles and guttural gurgling sounds.

Chapter 12

George's backpack was quickly ripped away, and before he grasped what was happening, he had already been dragged to one of the carved-out rooms and locked behind bars.

"Wait!" he cried. "You're supposed to help us, Spurlock!"

Lockerbie breezed through the bars and began barking at the group of goblins, but the goblins didn't seem to care. In fact, they began chanting...

"The GOBLINS will get you, if you don't watch out! The GOBLINS will get you, if you don't watch out! The GOBLINS will get you, if you don't watch out!"

George could feel the cold chills climb his spine. Hearing those chants from REAL goblins was the creepiest thing he had ever heard!

Spurlock pushed his way through the horde of goblins until he could stand directly in front of the bars between himself and George.

"I thought you were on our side," George blurted between Lockerbie's barks. "You said you hated the Goblin King!"

Spurlock tilted his head back and laughed. "I AM the GOBLIN KING!"

George stepped back, and Lockerbie did too.

"I knew I recognized his scent!" said Lockerbie. "But I didn't remember that silly suit!"

Spurlock's previous sing-song demeanor had completely shifted into something much more evil and vain. "FOOL!" he boomed. "You won't be cookin' up any spells down here, will ya?"

"What are you talking about?" said George.

"I knew as soon as I smelled you," said Spurlock. "You reek of Ewing Blood!"

"So, what?" said George as bravely as he could.

"Don't be coy!" Spurlock snapped. "You thought you'd be able to stop me like the other Ewing before you, but you're wrong!"

Lockerbie growled.

"And when I'm through," Spurlock spat, pointing to something behind George, "the world will be wiped away from all of that rubbish!"

George carefully turned his head to see what the Goblin King was pointing to. Behind him was a gigantic pile of books.

"GOLD!" said Spurlock, his words drenched in greed. "As soon as I unleash the Squee, those books will be swallowed and turned into precious metal."

"Is the humidor in here, too?" George prodded for more information.

"Did you hear that?" said Spurlock to the goblins. "This fool underestimates me!"

The goblins tightened around their leader. "Never underestimate the King," one lisped. "He will ssthmack you sssthilly, sssee..." This goblin smiled, showing a row of missing front teeth. The other goblins laughed hysterically.

"Silence," ordered Spurlock, lifting his fist and brandishing a big fat golden ring. "Or you'll all be missing YOUR teeth!"

Spurlock turned his attention back to George and Lockerbie. A wicked smile crossed his green face. "I've waited 99 years for Ewing blood," he said. "And now I have it, right here in my little lair. You're not the only one who can cast spells!"

This goblin thinks I can do magic, George thought to himself. Then an even more surprising thought entered his mind. Maybe he COULD do magic!

"All I need is a few drops of Ewing blood to reverse the spell," said Spurlock, rubbing his hands together. "Give me your finger!"

"Don't do it," said Lockerbie. She had finally stopped barking, although a continuous low growl rumbled from her throat.

"Never!" said George, stepping backwards toward the pile of stolen books.

He could hear the clinking of metal as a slender and much taller goblin pushed a key into the keyhole. But just as the key turned and made the clunking sound of an opened lock, George scooped up an armful of books and reached for Lockerbie's pink ribbon. Very quickly, he counted backwards from ten.

Chapter 13

"That was close!" said George, spilling the load of books onto Mr. Riley's bed.

"Well," said Lockerbie. "I'm happy that you remembered the ribbon. I was frozen with fear. All I could do was growl."

"We're a team," insisted George. "Without your magic ribbon, who knows what those goblins would have done to me."

George turned back to the books he had saved. He took note of all the titles and authors.

The Wonderful Wizard of Oz, by L. Frank Baum
Where the Sidewalk Ends, by Shel Silverstein
Where the Wild Things Are, by Maurice Sendack
Raggedy Ann Stories, by Johnny Gruelle
Little Women, by Louisa May Alcott
Sounder, by Wiliam H. Armstrong

"You saved some great literature," said Lockerbie.

"I've noticed something," said George, shuffling through the books. "I think all of these authors are dead."

Lockerbie sat on her haunches next to Mr. Riley's top hat. "You're right," she said. "That's my unfinished business."

"What do you mean by that?"

"The books of dead authors and poets who wrote for children produce more gold," explained Lockerbie. "Ten times more gold."

"I wonder why?" asked George.

"The way it was explained to me is that those who write for children 'have hearts of gold'," said Lockerbie. "Their legacies live on through the books they wrote."

George nodded. "Unless the goblins get ahold of them," he said.

"Precisely," said Lockerbie. "Any person who dedicates their lifework to the betterment of children has a heart of gold. And when they die, the only physical thing left is their words on paper. That's why it's turned to gold when the Squidgicum Squee swallows it."

"How did you learn this?"

"Mr. Riley, of course," Lockerbie insisted. "He and Mr. Ewing would spend many nights here in this bedroom discussing how they would stop the Squidgicum Squee."

George felt a tingling sensation rush up his arms, and for a moment he could've sworn he smelled snickerdoodle cookies.

"The Squidgicum Squee has taken many forms throughout the centuries," said Lockerbie. "Have you ever heard of Rumpelstiltskin?"

"Yes…"

"The Squidgicum Squee!"

"REALLY!?"

"King Midas?"

"Yes!"

"The Squidgicum Squee!"

"No way," shouted George.

"Its powers have changed over the centuries," said Lockerbie. "But one thing remains the same. It converts things into pure gold, and that power is never harnessed well by humans."

"Or goblins!"

"Precisely."

"Precisely, what?" said Judy, peeking her head around the doorframe. "Did you find the humidor?"

George and Lockerbie shared the details of their first trip down the Goblin Hole with Judy. They told her how they had been tricked by Spurlock and how he had tried to take George's blood for his own spell.

"You must have some magic in your blood if the Goblin King could smell it," said Judy. "That's probably why they practically tore down the door while your tour group was here the other day."

"Precisely," said Lockerbie. "And how did I not know that Spurlock was the Goblin King? I saw him once before."

"That was nearly a hundred years ago." said Judy.

"True," said Lockerbie. "And he certainly was not wearing that silly suit back then."

"There's one thing for sure, though," said Judy to

George. "The goblins have their sights on you. We must keep you protected."

"Precisely," said George.

"Hey, that's my word," said Lockerbie.

They all laughed, seeming to be delighted to have found some humor in their dire situation.

"You do say that word a lot," said George.

"I'm a precise poodle," Lockerbie insisted.

"A preciously precise poodle," said Judy with a giggle.

Just then, the front door buzzer sounded. "That's strange," said Judy. "It's Sunday. The museum's hours are precisely posted on the door."

They all crept downstairs to find out who was at the front door.

Chapter 14

George stood behind Judy as she unlocked the door. Lockerbie was stationed in the library with her head peeking around the corner. Judy slowly opened the door and found a lady staring back at her with a very serious look on her face.

"Granny!" George shouted as he ran toward the door. He scooted past Judy and pushed open the old fashioned storm door between them. "What are you doing here?" he said.

"Do you know what time it is?" said Granny. "Do you

know that I've been worried sick about you all day?"

George could see the tears welling in her eyes. He could also see that Granny was NOT in her housecoat. She was dressed in slacks as if she were going to church or the doctor.

"Come in, come in," said Judy. "Please, come in."

Granny handed George a ten dollar bill. "Run this out to the taxi driver, and tell him to keep the change."

George followed her directions, and when he came back inside, Granny and Judy were sitting on the fancy gold sofa in the drawing room.

"George," said Judy, standing up. "Keep your grandmother company while I fix us some coffee. We have lots to talk about."

Granny gave George a familiar look – a look that meant, "Child, you have some explaining to do."

While Judy was in the kitchen, Lockerbie breezed through the wall. Granny almost bounced out of her seat. "Must be the dog you mentioned in that note you left in the mailbox." she said.

"Poodle," Lockerbie corrected.

"We went down the Goblin Hole together," said George.

"Yes," said Granny. "We need to talk about that."

"You know something?" asked George, scooting to the edge of his seat.

"Years ago, I read about that hole." said Granny. "It's in the Book. It mentions Riley, but I didn't connect the dots until today."

Judy came back in the room with a silver coffee service. She placed it on the large table in the center of the room. "You take cream, Mrs. Ewing?"

"Yes," she answered. "But please call me, Betty. Only the doctor calls me Mrs. Ewing, yet I might need one after all of this."

George wasn't paying much attention to the small talk. He wanted his grandmother to share more about the Book.

Judy gave granny her coffee, and when everyone was seated again, Lockerbie spoke.

"Excuse me, Ms. Betty," she said. "Please tell us what you know."

"We have a book," she said. "In our family we refer to it as THE Book with a capital 'B'. It's full of family recipes and history, but it's also full of family charms and spells."

"Charms and spells!" said George. "Like magic?"

"You can call it magic, but I like to call it 'help'," said Granny with a wink. "It's a way of calling on our ancestors to assist in Earthly matters."

"Do you know much about this 'help', Betty?" said Lockerbie.

"Enough to get by," said Granny, "but my late husband was a practitioner of it and his parents before that. It's something that runs deep in the Ewing Family."

"What about the Squidgicum Squee spell?" asked George. "Is it in the Book?"

"It could be," said Granny, setting her cup and saucer on her lap. "But the most important part of that spell is right here in this room."

Lockerbie jumped on George's lap.

"That's right," said Granny to Lockerbie. "You and George."

"Fascinating," said Judy, taking a sip from her coffee.

"I'm certain that Lockerbie is the 'help' in this spell, and so are you, George," said Granny.

"That's right," said Lockerbie. "I've been waiting nearly one hundred years for you."

George looked at Lockerbie on his lap. He couldn't believe that he was a part of something so big. Just a few days ago, he was an ordinary kid, but now he was part of an extraordinary plan.

"Let's go see that Goblin Hole," said Granny.

"It's down in the basement," said George. "Are you sure you want to go down there?"

"You want more goblins to come out of that hole tonight?" she said.

"Absolutely not," said Judy. "But what are you going to do?"

"George's first lesson," she said.

Lockerbie led everyone down to the basement, and Judy showed Granny the Goblin Hole. Fortunately, the lid was tightly in place.

Granny pulled a red cloth pouch from her purse. "Brick dust," she said.

"We have that at the bottom of all our windows and doors," said George. "I just thought it kept the ants out."

"Keeps away more than bugs," said Granny as she bent over and sprinkled a big "X" over the lid. "Goblins are no different than any other kind of haint!"

"What's a haint?" asked George.

"Evil or dark spirit," explained Granny. "Something that wants to take instead of give."

"That's a good way to look at it," said Judy. "Those goblins are all about the taking and certainly no giving."

"George," said Granny, standing up. "I have a lot to teach you in very little time. But you've got the right blood or those goblins wouldn't be so scared of what you can do."

"Precisely," said Lockerbie. "He's got the same gift as Ewing, the Butler."

"Then tomorrow, I'll have to go back down there and find the humidor," said George. "Who knows what those goblins are cooking up? King Spurlock seems to have his own kind of magic, but he needs my blood to carry it out."

"Ain't no way he's getting my child's blood," said Granny, pulling George to her side. "Judy do you mind driving us home?"

"My pleasure," said Judy.

"I'll guard the house," said Lockerbie.

Chapter 15

Granny sat in the front, and George sat in the back of Judy's car. He had never ridden in such a fancy vehicle. Judy told him that it was a 1989 Fleetwood Cadillac with all of the bells and whistles. She had bought it brand new back then.

Judy started the engine and backed out of the museum's parking lot. She pulled down the alley that ran behind the museum and drove straight across East Street onto Vermont Street. George instantly remembered those streets on the signs in the goblin tunnels.

"Can we drive by the library?" asked George. "I want to

see what kind of building sits on top of the Goblin King's lair."

"Your wish is my command," said Judy as she pressed harder on the gas pedal. George could hear the strong purring of the engine as it floated down the road like a magic carpet. And as the car purred, George sat back in the plush velvet seats and almost fell asleep.

"Here it is," said Judy.

George straightened up.

"I used to come here when I was girl," said Granny. "The teachers at Crispus Attucks High would send us over here for research."

"Mr. Riley donated the land that this library sits on," said Judy. "His influence can be found all over the city."

"Like the hospital," said George. "That was named after him too, right?"

"Yes," said Judy. "After Mr. Riley died, a hospital for children was built in his honor."

"A heart of gold," George said as Judy pulled the car into a parking space.

"Did I ever tell you that your dad was a patient there, George," said Granny, turning her head to the backseat.

"No," said George, giving his grandmother a curious look. "There seems to be a lot of things you haven't told me."

Granny winked at him. "Well," she said, "they didn't charge us a dime."

"And they still don't," said Judy. "Riley Hospital provides free healthcare for children all over Indiana. Mr. Riley would be so proud."

"He'd be proud of that library too," said George. "It's gigantic!"

George gazed at the large stone building. The huge columns reminded him of something he might see in ancient Greece. Then he remembered what lay beneath that stately and heavy looking building – the lair of the Goblin King. This also reminded George of the task that lay before him.

"If you have time," said Judy. "I can take you by the hospital so George can see it."

"Sure," said Granny. "I haven't been by there in years."

Granny hasn't been by anything in years, George thought to himself. He was still surprised that she was in the front seat of Judy's car – in regular clothes!

Judy pulled out of her parking space and eased down St. Clair Street, turning right onto Meridian Street. Just a few blocks up, she turned left onto 10th Street. They traveled down 10th all the way to the Riley Hospital for Children.

"That's a big place," said George, looking at the multileveled glass and brick building.

Judy drove her Cadillac around the main entrance of the building, giving George and Granny a view of the inside.

"The original façade of the 1924 building is preserved in the atrium," said Judy.

"I remember that," said Granny. "When Denny would come back for his check-ups, we'd ride the glass elevator, and we'd throw pennies into the fountain by the bench with Riley's statue."

"It's all still there," said Judy.

"All for us kids," said George. "What a special place."

Judy drove her car back out onto 10th Street and turned left onto West Street, which eventually became MLK Street. They passed the darkened landscapes of Crown Hill Cemetery and pulled into Granny's driveway.

"Thanks for the ride, Judy," said Granny, "George has lots to learn tonight, but don't worry about the Goblin Hole. The brick dust will keep it sealed."

"I'll take your word for it," she said. "Brick dust seems

more effective and less expensive than pickles."

"Pickles?" Granny blurted.

"George can tell you about that," Judy laughed. "Lockerbie and I will watch over the museum tonight."

George got out first and helped Granny from her seat, but before he shut the door, Judy reminded him of Mr. Riley's words, "The goblins will get you if you don't watch out!"

"Ha!" said George. "Ain't that the truth."

Chapter 16

George followed Granny into her bedroom. He had been in there hundreds of times and had seen the small table with all of the candles and old photos on it, but he had never paid it much attention. Granny's special stones and crystals were displayed on the table too, along with the Book.

"Our dearly departed," said Granny as she struck a match and lit one of the candles.

George's eyes landed on a photo of his mother. She was seated on Granny's front porch with a book in her lap. He picked it up and ran his fingers over the polished wooden frame.

"They're all framed in Ebony," Granny explained. "Wood from Africa."

George picked up another photo. It appeared to be a young couple on their wedding day.

"My mother and father," said Granny. "They died a long time ago."

As George placed the photos back in their positions, he felt goosebumps travel down his arms. Granny must have seen him shiver.

"They're letting you know they're here," she said. "And that's a good thing since we'll be calling on their help tonight."

Just then the candle began to flicker as if someone was blowing on it.

"That's my mother," said Granny. "She blows on the candle to let me know she's here. She's been doing that ever since I got robbed that day."

"Does Dad know about all of this?" asked George.

"He'd rather joke about it," Granny explained. "But he does."

George picked up the Book and held it to his chest. He could feel something inside of himself shift. He felt wiser and older, but even more than that, he felt connected.

"Wherever I go, they are with me," he said. "Whenever I'm alone or scared, I don't have to be because my family is here."

Granny put her arm around George and squeezed him close. "Lesson number one," she said, "and you passed. Now bring the Book to the kitchen, and I'll fix us something to eat."

At the kitchen table, George flipped through the pages. There were recipes for everything. Some of them were written directly on the brown paper, while others looked like they had been clipped from newspapers and pasted in. The first one that caught his eye was a banana pudding recipe. That was a Thanksgiving favorite in his family.

Then, George noticed a section filled with a different type of recipes called charms and spells. As George leafed through these pages, savory smells of onions, bell peppers and celery filled the room.

"Jambalaya?" said George, raising his nose from the charms and spells.

"Child, if we are working magic, we need to eat the right food," Granny replied.

Granny's Jambalaya was another one of George's favorites. His stomach growled, but he pulled his attention away from the food and back to the Book. He turned another page, and there it was. In big, bold letters it said, SQUIDGICUM SQUEE VACUUM SPELL.

"Found it!" George exclaimed.

"Just a second, let me get a lid for this," said Granny. She opened the cupboard beneath the counter next to the kitchen stove. "Actually, can you reach in there, George? It's way back in there."

George left the Book on the kitchen table and approached Granny's dark and deep cabinets. She had once told him that most old houses had roomy cabinets like that. They were so roomy that George used to crawl inside and hide in them when he didn't want to go home. This was when he'd spend weekends with Granny before his mom had died.

Reaching into the cabinet, George didn't feel any lids. He felt something warm and...

"OUCH!" he yelled. "Something bit me!"

That something was a GOBLIN, and it leapt out of the cabinet and darted across the room.

"Lord, help us!" yelled Granny.

The goblin looked back at them with a toothy smile. He was carrying a handkerchief with what looked like a little bloodstain on it.

George looked down at his finger. "I'm bleeding!"

Just then, the goblin snatched the Book from the table and zinged across the living room toward the fireplace. George and Granny chased after him, but before they could reach him, he was already shimmying up the chimney. The claws on his toes tore into the soot, causing a puff of black smoke to blow into the room.

"He's got the Book," George yelled. "And my blood!"

Chapter 17

"Who knows what kinds of germs and diseases those awful things carry," said Granny. She had taken George into the bathroom. "Hold still," she said as she poured hydrogen peroxide over George's hand. The goblin had bitten him on the flesh between his thumb and pointer finger.

"This isn't good," said George as the peroxide bubbled on his wound. "The goblins have everything they need to reverse the spell, and I have no clue how to stop them."

"Without the Book, we'll have to wing-it," said Granny.

She blotted the wound with a clean washcloth to soak up the excess peroxide and what little blood was still flowing. Once it was mostly dry, she quickly placed a Band-Aid over the bite mark. "That should do it," she said.

George's thoughts were lightyears away from the pain he felt in his hand. He tried to remember the words of the spell he was looking at before Granny had asked him to reach for the lid, but all he could recall was the title.

"The first thing we'll need is a protection charm," said Granny. "No one is going back down that hole without one."

"How do we make one of those?" asked George.

"Graveyard dirt," said Granny.

"Well, that's easy," said George. "We live next to the third largest graveyard in the country."

"It's a delicate operation, though. It takes concentration and money."

"Money?" said George. "How much?"

"A dime," said Granny, "for each grave you take from. Otherwise that spirit can't put their help into the dirt."

George was surprised with Granny's knowledge on this topic. He was used to her special crystals and stones, but this was a whole different ballgame.

"But we're not going to be useful without something to eat," she said. "How about some jambalaya?"

Granny dished them each a bowl, and as soon as she set the bowls on the table, George dug in. He could taste the blend of garlic, parsley and thyme. The shrimp were sweet, and the tomatoes had cooked nicely into the fluffy rice.

"Once we're through eating," said Granny, "we'll have to sneak into the cemetery."

"In the dark?" said George, lifting his head from his bowl.

"That's the best time to do it."

"If you say so," said George.

The two of them finished their Jambalaya and began washing the dishes. As soon as Granny started humming, George recognized the song she was about to sing. It was the song she had sung to him since he was a baby - *Ain't No Mountain High Enough*. This song was about LOVE and how nothing could get in its way. Granny took her wet and soapy hands out of the sink and grabbed George's arm. She spun him around and grabbed his hands. As they sang, they danced around the kitchen floor. And when they finished singing, Granny bent over and kissed George on the forehead.

"Why are we washing these dishes, anyway?" she said. "We have bigger fish to fry, don't we?"

"They're called goblins," said George, "with piranha-sharp teeth."

They dried their hands and gathered the items they'd need for the cemetery: a flashlight, a spoon, a few dimes and a small cast iron pot.

But before they went out into the night, Granny pulled out the pouch of brick dust and sprinkled a line at the foot of the fireplace. "I never thought one would come down the chimney," she said. "But when you know better, you do better."

"I don't get it," said George. "How does brick dust work?"

"Think about it," said Granny. "What are bricks made for?"

"To build stuff…"

"And what are we trying to build here?"

George thought about it for a moment. "A wall?" he said.

"That's right," said Granny with a smirk. "You're learnin' fast."

"I still don't understand how it works," said George. "Does any old brick dust repel evil?"

"No," said Granny. "It must come from the dwelling of an ancestor."

"Where did yours come from?" asked George.

"The house I grew up in was torn down about thirty years ago," said Granny. "Grandpa George and I went over there afterwards and took a small load of bricks. I've got enough to last my lifetime and yours."

"Well, that's comforting," said George as he followed Granny to the backdoor.

They turned out the lights, except the one over the kitchen sink and left the house. George couldn't believe that his grandmother had left twice in the same day.

"It's a full moon," said Granny as they walked down the street towards the southwest corner of the cemetery. "The spirits are awake tonight."

George wondered if he would see the spirit of James Whitcomb Riley again, or maybe he and Granny would pass President Benjamin Harrison and his wife taking an evening stroll. They were buried there too, along with the notorious gangster John Dillinger and Granny's favorite poet, Etheridge Knight. In the back of George's mind, there was always the hope that he might see his mom. She was buried there too.

All that thinking and wondering brought the southwest corner to their feet mighty quickly. "There's the hole in the fence," said George, pointing to his secret entrance. "This is where I met Lockerbie the other day."

"Child, how am I going to squeeze through that?"

George slipped right through and held the flap of chain-link fencing above his head so that the hole was tall enough for granny to squeeze through without having to crawl.

"We've got to be careful," she said. "Who knows who

else might be in here this time of night."

George knew that was right. He remembered his dad mentioning that people who lived on the streets would often sleep in the cemetery. The thought of sleeping amongst the gravestones shot goosebumps up his arms and down his back.

"Don't turn the flashlight on," said Granny, leading the way. "I don't think we'll need it with a moon this bright."

They passed the spruce trees and the rock that Lockerbie had sat on, and they crossed the road that traced the outer portion of the cemetery. "I know where you are taking me," said George. "Dad and I visit her grave all the time."

"Does that mean you want to lead the way?" Granny's smirk was highlighted in the moon's glow.

George walked just a few paces ahead when he noticed a pair of headlights cruising around the trees. "Security!" he said. "Get behind that tree."

George pointed to the giant oak tree ahead of them. They quickly ducked behind it and let the security truck pass. George looked up at the moon and released a sigh. "That was close," he said.

Turning his attention back to his mother's grave, George and Granny continued walking. It wasn't much further – just over another small cemetery road.

"Look for the angel," said Granny.

"It's right there," he said. "I've been here a hundred times."

"Don't get sassy with me, child," said Granny. "I'll conjure a whole mess of ghosts to chase your little behind home."

George couldn't help but giggle. He waited for Granny to catch up, and they made the final few steps together. His mother's stone was truly beautiful, especially in the light of the moon. Her name was etched inside a blue granite heart with guardian angels on each side.

Wendy Alyce Ewing
1981 - 2011
Loving Mother and Wife

"Your dad worked six months of overtime to buy your mom's stone," said Granny. "He wanted the best."

"It is the best," said George.

George's dad had also planted a ginkgo tree a few feet from the stone. Each autumn the leaves would turn a golden yellow and drop overnight, leaving a carpet of color over Wendy's grave.

Granny put her hand on George's shoulder. "Okay," she said, "dig beneath the grass and get some good dirt. And while you're digging, think about your mom – only good memories, nothing sad. Then, place this dime in the hole."

George took the spoon and small pot from Granny. "That's all I do?"

"That's it," said Granny.

As George dug into the dirt, he thought about the time his mom had taken him to the zoo. He remembered feeding the giraffes and watching the elephants splash around in the water. They ate ice cream cones and watched the monkeys play, and when they reached the gift shop, his mom let him choose a book. George picked one about giraffes. That night, she read it to him before bed. Giraffes had been his favorite animal ever since.

"That's enough dirt," said Granny, pulling George away from his thoughts.

Granny handed him the dime, and as he placed it into the hole, it shined in the moonlight. As he stood up, he kissed his hand and touched his mother's stone. He and his dad always did that whenever they left her grave.

George followed Granny over a little hill. It didn't take him very long to figure out that they were headed to Grandpa George's grave.

"I haven't been here in twenty years," she said. "I miss him so much."

George heard Granny sniffling and saw a shiny tear drop from her cheek. Her body shook with each quiet sob. George placed the pot and spoon on the ground and grabbed Granny's hand.

"I should've come here sooner," she said. "There is no sense in me staying holed up in that house and mad at the world."

"You're here, now, Granny," George told her, squeezing her hand. "And I'm here with you."

"I know you are, honey," she said, wiping the tears from her eyes. "And I'm glad about that. Now, let's get to work."

They repeated the same ritual, except they switched roles. Granny scooped the dirt, since she was the one with the happy memories of Grandpa George. And when they were finished, they headed north, up Crown Hill.

"Are we going where I think we're going?" asked George.

"We need something special from his grave," said Granny. "Have any idea what it is?"

"Pennies?"

"You're catching on quick, Mr. Magic!"

They walked very slowly up the nicely paved road to Mr. Riley's tomb. Granny tugged on George's arm and stopped about halfway. "We gotta slow down, child," she said. "This hill is steep."

George stopped and turned around to see how far they had walked. That's when he saw the most spectacular sight.

"Granny, look!" he said. "Indianapolis at night!"

Crown Hill was the highest point in the city, and since it was nearly four miles from downtown, the view of the skyline was breathtaking.

"Look at the giant robot!" shouted George. "It's all lit up."

"Robot?" said Granny, catching her breath. "Where do you see a robot?"

"The tallest building! Can't you see it?"

Granny started laughing. "Why, I guess it does look like a robot with those two big antennas coming out the top!"

George looked to the left of the skyline and tried imagining where the museum was. This made him wonder about Judy and Lockerbie. He hoped that they were okay and that the brick dust was still blocking the Goblin Hole.

Granny turned back toward the hill and put one foot in front of the other. George followed her lead all the way up the steps of Mr. Riley's tomb, but someone else had beaten them there.

Chapter 18

"Get back," yelled Granny, shielding George from the goblin. "You ain't getting no more blood from him."

The goblin stepped out of the shadows and onto the marble slab in the center of Mr. Riley's tomb. The moonlight brightened its green skin, and George could see that it was wearing a red and white polka dotted dress. It was a girl.

"I come in peace," she said with her palms out. "I was hoping that I would find you here."

George and Granny stood in silence, but the goblin kept

talking.

"They would lock me up if they knew I was here," she said. "But I want to help you."

"Help us?" asked George. "Why?"

"Not all goblins are bad," she said. "Most of us are peaceful, but King Spurlock's crew forces us to steal books. He threatens to feed us to the Squee if we don't."

"But the Squidgicum Squee is locked in the humidor," said George. "He couldn't feed you to it if he tried."

"That's right," said the goblin. "But we live for hundreds of years, and we all know that King Spurlock will release the Squee sooner or later."

George placed the pot filled with graveyard dirt on the ground and crossed his arms. "How do I know your aren't lying?"

"That's right," said Granny. "How do we know?"

The goblin jumped off the slab and reached for something in the bushes. "Here," she said, throwing George his backpack. "I believe this belongs to you."

George recognized his backpack immediately, but it was heavier than what he remembered. He opened it and found that it was filled with books.

"I got your books plus some more," said the goblin. "I hope that shows whose side I'm on."

"What's your name?" said George.

"Violet," she answered, grabbing the bottom of her polka dotted dress with a curtsy.

"That doesn't sound like a goblin kind of name to me," said Granny.

"We're not all brutes and savages," said Violet. "Some of us are quite sophisticated."

"Nice to meet you, Violet," said George, extending his hand. "And thank you for saving these books."

Violet shook his hand. "The pleasure is all mine."

After a few moments of reluctance, Granny finally extended her hand. "Violet," she said. "It's nice to meet you."

After the pleasantries, Granny instructed George to place a dime amongst all of the pennies on Mr. Riley's tomb. It had been a tradition since Mr. Riley's death for people to put pennies on his grave to be scooped up and donated to the hospital.

"Now take three pennies as change," said Granny. "These will go inside the charm bags with the graveyard dirt."

"Working a spell?" asked Violet.

"Eye of newt and a goblin tooth," said Granny with a wink. "Just kidding."

"Funny," said Violet, although she wasn't laughing. "Goblins have been talking about Ewing blood for nearly a hundred years."

"You don't look more than twelve," said Granny.

"Goblins age very slowly," said Violet. "I'm actually a hundred and twelve."

"One-hundred and twelve?" said George with wide eyes.

"That's right," said Violet. "And Riley and Ewing's Century Spell is legendary in our world. You see, most of the goblins were happy to see the Squee sucked up by a spell and locked into that little box."

"And now the Goblin King has it once again," said George.

"Yes," said Violet. "But I know where it's hidden."

"You do? Can you take us there?" said George.

"That's why I'm here," said Violet.

George couldn't help but wonder if he was being bamboozled once again by a goblin, but there was certainly something different about Violet. She did seem quite demure and peaceful. And he wondered what her motive would be to lure him back underground anyway. The goblins already had the Book and his blood. That thought shook George into action.

"We've got to go," he said. "We're running out of time!"

Chapter 19

"She's telling the truth," said Granny as all three of them entered the back door of her house. "Nothing evil can cross the dust."

George looked down and saw the red brick dust that Violet had just walked over with no problem. The previous goblin had to come down the chimney to get in, so George believed that his grandmother's evaluation was correct.

"You two have a seat at the kitchen table," said Granny. "I'll be right back."

George thought it was funny that she was treating Violet like she was just another friend he had invited over from school. It was still hard to believe that Violet was a hundred and twelve years old.

"So, who's the lady with all the pickles?" asked Violet?

"That's Judy," he said. "She is the historian at the museum where the Squidicum Squee had been for nearly a hundred years."

"Mincemeat," said Violet. "We love to eat anything pickled, but mincemeat will put us to sleep."

"Cold mince pies," said George. "Mr. Riley wrote about those in his nine little goblins poem."

To his amazement, Violet recited the whole thing.

They all climbed up on a high board-fence —
Nine little Goblins with green-glass eyes —
Nine little Goblins that had no sense,
And couldn't tell coppers from cold mince pies;
And they all climbed up on the fence, and sat —
And I asked them what they were staring at.

And the first one said, as he scratched his head
With a queer little arm that reached out of his ear
And rasped its claws in his hair so red —
"This is what this little arm is fer!"
And he scratched and stared, and the next one said
"How on earth do you scratch your head?"

And he laughed like the screech of a rusty hinge —
Laughed and laughed till his face grew black;
And when he choked, with a final twinge
Of his stifling laughter, he thumped his back
With a fist that grew on the end of his tail
Till the breath came back to his lips so pale.

And the third little Goblin leered round at me —
And there were no lids on his eyes at all —
And he clucked one eye, and he says, says he,
"What is the style of your socks this fall?"
And he clapped his heels — and I sighed to see
That he had hands where his feet should be.

Then a bald-faced Goblin, gray and grim,
Bowed his head, and I saw him slip
His eyebrows off, as I looked at him,
And paste them over his upper lip;
And then he moaned in remorseful pain —
"Would — Ah, would I'd me brows again!"
And then the whole of the Goblin band
Rocked on the fence-top to and fro,
And clung, in a long row, hand in hand,
Singing the songs that they used to know —
Singing the songs that their grandsires sung
In the goo-goo days of the Goblin-tongue.

And ever they kept their green-glass eyes
Fixed on me with a stony stare —
Till my own grew glazed with a dread surmise,
And my hat whooped up on my lifted hair,
And I felt the heart in my breast snap-to
As you've heard the lid of a snuff-box do.
And they sang, "You're asleep! There is no board-fence,
And never a Goblin with green-glass eyes! —
'Tis only a vision the mind invents
After a supper of cold mince-pies, —
And you're doomed to dream this way," they said, —
And you sha' n't wake up till you're clean plum dead!

Violet must have read the astonished look on George's face. "Most goblins know that one," she said. "I like 'Little Orphant Annie' too."

Just then, Granny returned with a pair of scissors and a red shirt. "Red flannel," she said. "It was your grandpa's. It took a while to find it, but I knew it was in that closet somewhere."

"Why do we need his shirt?" asked George.

"Not just any shirt," she insisted. "To make charm bags, you must use red flannel, and since this was your grandpa's, it'll work that much better."

Granny handed George the scissors. "Cut three pretty good sized squares out of the back," she said.

She then scooted the cast iron pot closer to George. "When you're through with that, drop a scoop of graveyard dirt in the center of each square."

George followed Granny's instructions as Violet watched intently. Granny got up from the table and went back to her room. She brought a spool of cotton string and a dried rose back to the table.

"Granny, what are you doing with your special rose?" asked George.

"A special rose for a special charm," she said as she carefully removed three petals.

George knew then that Granny was not playing around. If she was taking apart her special rose, then this magic business was serious.

"You still have those pennies?" she asked? "Put one on each mound of dirt?"

As George arranged the pennies, Granny placed a rose petal on top of them.

"Now, shake some salt on each one," Granny instructed.

"What does salt do?" asked George.

"Just like any recipe," said Granny, "you add salt to bring out the flavor."

When George was finished with that, Granny showed him how to gather each bag's four corners and tie them together with string.

"Charm bags," she said, bouncing them gently in her hand. "Nothing will harm us now."

Granny asked George to go ahead and put one of the charms in his pocket. Almost instantly, he felt his leg get warmer, then his whole body. But it wasn't like the heat from a fire. It felt like he had stepped into a warm and comfortable bath.

Then, out of nowhere, Lockerbie appeared in the doorway between the kitchen and living room. "We're keeping company with goblins again, I see," she said.

Granny gasped and jerked her head toward the poodle. "You spooked me!"

"Well, I am a ghost," said Lockerbie. "We do tend to spook."

"This is Violet," said George. "She is on our side."

"I believe we've been down this trail before," said Lockerbie. "The last goblin we trusted tried to imprison you, remember?"

"She crossed the brick dust," said Granny. "Nothing of ill will could've done that."

"And she returned my backpack and books, plus some," added George.

Once George was finally able to convince Lockerbie that Violet was on their side, he explained to Violet that Lockerbie was a ghost-poodle and the famous canine companion to James Whitcomb Riley.

"Well, I have bad news," said Lockerbie. "I'm afraid the goblins have found a new entrance into the museum."

"Brick dust," said Granny. We should've circled the

whole house."

"But don't they have what they want?" asked George?

"They're after a piece of Mr. Riley's clothing," said Violet. "Something like a glove or hat..."

"The top hat!" Lockerbie shouted. "And I've left it on the bed - UNGUARDED!"

Granny grabbed the other two charm bags from the kitchen table. "You got any old bricks lying around that basement?" she asked.

"Several," said Lockerbie, "from the original carriage house that Mr. and Mrs. Ewing lived in."

"Bingo!" said Granny, rummaging through a kitchen drawer. She pulled out a hammer. "Let's pound some bricks!"

"George," said Violet. "Don't forget about the mincemeat."

"Mincemeat?" said Lockerbie. "Why does that sound familiar?"

"It puts goblins to sleep," said George. "Do you know how to make it, Granny?"

"Child," she said. "I can make mincemeat with my eyes closed."

"Well, looks like we'll be busy tonight," said George, pulling the ribbon from Lockerbie's hair and counting backwards from ten.

Chapter 20

George wasn't sure if Lockerbie's ribbon would work on all three of them, but it did. They were immediately transported to Mr. Riley's bedroom.

"Hallelujah!" Lockerbie shouted. "The hat is still here."

"That's a relief," said George, noticing the undisturbed top hat resting on Mr. Riley's bed. "Let's find Judy."

Everyone followed George down the back stairway to the kitchen. Judy wasn't there. They called her name and worked their way to the front of the house where they found the front door wide open. George could hear Judy's voice.

"Get!" she yelled. "Get outa here!"

Outside, Judy was throwing pickles at a gang of goblins from the steps near the sidewalk, but she couldn't feed them fast enough.

"Judy!" George yelled, looking around for neighbors. "We need your help!"

Luckily, nobody was out and about on Lockerbie Street. Some lights were on inside of the houses, but the street was quiet.

Granny had already reached for the pouch of brick dust in her purse and sprinkled some across the front doorway. "They won't be crossing here."

Once Judy was back inside, George shut the door tightly. "How did they get in?" he asked her.

"Down the chimney right into the library!" she said with hands dripping with pickle juice. "What else are they after?"

"One came down my chimney and hid in my kitchen cupboards," said Granny. "George reached in to get a lid, and the darned thing bit him. Took his blood on a hankie."

"To reverse the spell," said Lockerbie. "Now all they need is the top hat."

"Goblins are persistent," said Violet, stepping out from behind the hall tree. "The good ones and the bad ones."

Judy jumped back and grabbed a pickle from her pocket.

"She's with us," said George. "We've already questioned her."

"And she passed the brick dust," said Granny. "No evil bone in her body."

Judy placed the pickle back inside her pocked and gave a sigh of relief. "I like your polka dots," she said.

"I like yours too," said Violet, smiling. "By the way,

pickles only make us crazy. Mincemeat puts us to sleep."

Judy scratched her head. "That's right," she said. "Mr. Riley wrote that in a poem. How did we forget, Lockerbie?"

"Precisely," said Lockerbie. "So much to remember."

"When you know better, you do better," said George, looking at Granny.

"That's right," said Granny. "Now, about those pies... Is there a working oven in this old house?"

"We'll have to fire up the wood stove, but that won't be an easy task," said Judy, wrinkling her brow. "Fortunately, we do have a woodpile left behind from a tree that fell this spring."

"Do you realize how many pies we'll have to make, though?" said George. "There's a whole lot of goblins down there."

Judy scratched her head again. "That's true," she said. "And pies aren't easy to carry..."

"Wait," said Lockerbie. "I do remember something! Nannie Ewing, the butler's wife, made mincemeat cookies."

"Perfect," said George looking at Granny with wide eyes!

"I've seen that recipe," said Granny. "It's in the Book. I've made them once or twice. We can use jarred mincemeat from the store."

"Great," said George. "Can you and Judy run to the store while we grind the brick dust?"

"There's a market a few blocks away," said Judy, "on New Jersey and Vermont. Let me grab my keys."

While Judy went for her keys, Granny handed George the hammer she had brought from her house. George, Violet and Lockerbie listened to Granny's instructions on how to grind bricks into magic brick dust.

"While grinding the dust, imagine a big ball of bright light surrounding you," she insisted. "This bright light will repel all evil and will charm the dust."

"How?" said George.

"It's all about intention, just like we made the charms," she said. "Think of it that way."

Judy returned with her keys, and she and Granny walked out the front door. The goblins must have retreated because they were nowhere in sight.

Lockerbie lead George and Violet downstairs to a pile of old bricks from the original carriage house. "I remember when they tore it down," she said. "Luckily, these bricks were saved."

George picked up one and rubbed his hands across the rough surface. He closed his eyes and imagined a big ball of bright light. He wasn't expecting a face to appear in the center.

Chapter 21

"That is a spirit, not a ghost," said Lockerbie.

George opened his eyes and was surprised to see a man standing before them. He was tall and slender and glowed like Lockerbie.

"Lockerbie," said the man. "It's been a long time."

"Dennis Ewing…the Butler?" said Lockerbie. "What a surprise!"

George's mouth hung wide open as he stared at his 5th great grandfather's apparition.

"Grandson," said the Butler. "I'm here to help you."

George looked closely at his ancestor. He didn't look like a butler at all. Butlers were supposed to wear tuxedos with tails and carry silver trays. This man's clothes were nice but ordinary. He wore regular brown pants with a white button-up shirt and brown jacket. His shoes were brown and ordinary, too.

"There's an enchanted bottle buried in the backyard near the poplar tree," said the Butler. "For a hundred years it's been waiting for you."

"Me?" said George, pointing to himself.

"That's right, grandson," said the Butler. "You've been part of this plan since you were just a star the sky."

"How?" said George, stepping closer to the glowing apparition.

"Destiny," said the Butler. "You've got the magic in your blood."

George took a deep breath and exhaled very slowly. "But I don't' know how to..."

"Trust your heart," said the Butler.

Just as George was about to ask another question, the Butler faded away. "I'm so proud of you," he said. And those were his final words.

George stood in silence for a moment. "Did that just happen or am I losing my mind?" he asked.

"It happened," said Violet. "Wow!"

"The bottle!" said Lockerbie. "I know where it's buried."

As they discussed the bottle, Violet proceeded to pound a brick into dust. As she was sweeping it into a brown paper sack, she suddenly stopped. "Listen," she said, pointing a slender green finger towards the ceiling. "Do you hear that?"

The sound of footsteps crept along the floorboards

above them. "Sounds like a..." Lockerbie began.

"Goblin," George finished. "Bring the brick dust."

Once again, Lockerbie led the way. She breezed through a wall and quickly came back with a confirmation. "Goblin, indeed!" she said.

George and Violet stormed through the basement door and rounded the corner towards the breakfast room. Sure enough, a goblin had entered the house. He was much taller than the usual two feet. This brute was huge, and he was practically naked – only wearing what looked like a small pair of underwear.

"Bobo!" shouted Violet. "Stop!"

This caught the goblin off guard. He had already made it to the backdoor, but he quickly turned around. "V-v-violet?" he stuttered. His voice was low but childish.

"Put it down," she said.

The goblin was holding Mr. Riley's hat.

"S-s-sorry," he said, twisting the knob, but the door was locked. "K-k-king Spurlock made me do it."

"Bobo!" Violet shouted again. "Put down the hat!"

With that, Bobo yanked at the knob and pulled the whole door off its hinges. "S-s-sorry," he said again, lurching into the darkness.

Lockerbie chased after him. Her barks pierced the night. A bedroom light flipped on in a house across the alley.

"What are we going to do?" said George.

"Oh...my," said a voice behind them. "What happened to the door?"

George turned around to find Judy and his grandmother back from the store. They both held shopping bags.

"They got the top hat," said George in a defeated tone. "And Lockerbie is chasing the goblin who stole it."

Granny and Judy placed the groceries on the kitchen's hardwood floors.

"She'll come back," said Judy. "We just have to work extra fast now."

"Lightning fast," said Granny.

"What about the brick dust?" said Violet. "I doubt we even need it now."

"Better safe than sorry," said Granny, taking the sack from Violet and emptying it into her red pouch.

"I'm already feeling pretty sorry," said George, hanging his head.

But then he remembered the apparition of Ewing, the Butler and his words of encouragement. He realized that there was no time to feel defeated. His intuition was telling him to dig up that bottle and use it to trap the Squidgicum Squee once and for all. History depended on him!

Chapter 22

Granny and Judy had already begun making the mincemeat cookies when they sent George and Violet outside for wood. They walked down the brick pathway and turned left into the spacious lawn and gardens next to the museum. George kept an eye out for Lockerbie, but he also looked for a century old poplar tree.

"That's it," he said, pointing to the massive tree. "The leaves are shaped like tulips, see?"

"What are you talking about?" asked Violet. She had already found the woodpile and was holding an armful of wood. She was a small goblin, but she was mighty.

"The tulip poplar is the Indiana State Tree," said George. "The enchanted bottle must be buried under it."

"It's huge," said Violet. "And look! There's a chain hanging from it, too."

"I wonder why," said George.

Violet dropped the wood and ran to the tree. In no time, she had climbed the chain to the top, but as quickly as she had climbed up, she climbed back down.

"Hurry, grab that wood!" she said. "We're not alone."

That's when George saw the goblins sliding down the chain – a lot of them. George scooped up the armload of wood and rushed through the kitchen doorway. Violet was close behind.

"Throw me that brick dust," yelled George.

As soon as Granny tossed him the brick dust, he sprinkled a line across the doorway just in time. He counted nine little goblins crawling and climbing over each other, trying to get past the line. They were the strangest creatures he had ever seen. One had an arm that reached out of his ear. Another had a fist at the end of his tail, and they all had bright red hair.

"Can you believe it?" said Judy. "Those are the goblins from Mr. Riley's poem."

"They came down a chain in the tree," said George.

"They're comedians," said Violet. "They entertain King Spurlock every night in the lair."

"What could they want from us?" said Granny.

"They probably smell the mincemeat," explained Violet. "I'm sure they've been waiting up in that tree for the perfect time to pounce."

Granny scooped some cold mincemeat from a jar. "Take that!" she said, flinging it out the doorway and into the swarm of green skin and red hair.

George could hear the slurps and grunts of joy. Then, almost instantly, the goblins mellowed. They sat down and looked into the kitchen with satisfied eyes. A few seconds later they were asleep and snoring.

George maneuvered himself through the sleeping goblins and ran back to the woodpile for another armload, and when he returned, he helped place the door back on it hinges. The door needed some maintenance, but it covered the doorway nonetheless.

"I haven't fired up a wood stove since I was a girl in Virginia," said Judy. "Grandma had a stove just like this at the farm."

George handed Judy a few small sticks of wood. She placed those inside the stove with some newspaper and struck a match. Bright orange and yellow flames licked the newspaper. Within minutes the sounds of crackling wood filled the kitchen. Judy closed the stove door and pointed to a small thermometer.

"When it gets to three-fifty, we'll put the cookies in," she said.

"Simple enough," said George.

"You two come over here and ball-up this dough," said Granny, holding up an example. "I'll finish sprinkling the brick dust."

George and Violet rolled the dough and placed the little balls on a cookie sheet. Judy went behind them and flattened the cookies with the bottom of a drinking glass.

When the oven was hot enough, Judy opened the stove door, and George slid in the first batch of mincemeat cookies. As they baked, the kitchen filled with the sweet scents of warm butter and hot candied fruits and spices.

"They smell almost as good as snickerdoodles," said George.

Violet wiped a small amount of drool from the corner

of her mouth. "I should probably go help Granny," she said. "I'm feeling drowsy."

But before she could go anywhere, Granny came down the kitchen stairs. "It's Lockerbie," she said. "She's on Mr. Riley's bed in pretty bad shape."

Chapter 23

Judy rushed to Lockerbie's side. "Why are you crying, my dear?" she said.

"Mr. Riley's hat is gone," she sniffled. "I tried to fetch it, but I ran too far from the room."

"Too far from the room?" asked George.

"There are only certain things that Lockerbie can physically touch," explained Judy. "Everything in this room is part of Lockerbie's domain, but the further something is taken from this room, the less power Lockerbie has to protect it."

By now, everyone was standing around Mr. Riley's bed, trying to console Lockerbie. She had curled herself into a little ball with her paws covering her eyes. Her glow had dimmed to a much fainter light, making her difficult to see.

"Lockerbie," said George. "Help me find the enchanted bottle, and we'll go together to get Mr. Riley's hat."

"The what bottle?" asked Granny.

"I haven't had time to tell you," said George. "Ewing, the Butler visited us while you and Judy were gone to the store, and he told me about an enchanted bottle he buried years ago."

"You saw him?" asked Granny

"Just like Mr. Riley at the recital," said George.

Lockerbie's whimpers quieted, and her glow appeared to brighten. She sat up on the bed. "I'll take you to the bottle," she said. "I know where it is."

Granny interrupted Lockerbie. "What else did he say?" she asked.

"He told me that I have magic in my blood, and that I'll know how to use it," explained George. "And I believe I do."

"Tell us," said Judy.

"The Butler's bottle will trap the Squidgicum Squee once and for all!" said George.

"Nothin' but an old haint," said Granny, nodding.

"A what?" asked Violet.

"An old haint," said Lockerbie. "That's what Ewing, the Butler had called it too."

"Just another word for ghost - the kind that haunts," said Granny, winking at Lockerbie. "Not the kind that helps."

"Precisely," said Lockerbie. Her brightness had completely restored.

"If this bottle is so powerful," said George. "I wonder why it wasn't used to trap the Squidgicum Squee in the first place, though."

Granny took a seat in Mr. Riley's desk chair and explained. "Our kind of magic is personal," she said. "Objects used in spells must have a connection to the one in need. The humidor belonged to Mr. Riley, right?"

"It sure did," said Judy.

"That's why Ewing, the Butler chose the humidor, since it was a special possession of Mr. Riley. It also had the same purpose as a bottle - to contain or trap things."

"Would any old bottle work?" asked Violet, curiously.

"By someone who knows what they're doing," said Granny. "But this bottle sounds very different."

"Ewing, the Butler buried it for George to find a century later," said Lockerbie. "It was all part of the original spell. I remember, now."

"The bottle must be charmed," said Granny. "And it's had a hundred years to charge, so to speak."

"Like a battery?" asked George.

"I guess you could say that"

"Well," said Violet. "I don't want to alarm you, but Bobo has had time to make it back to the lair. They will start reversing the spell anytime now."

"She's right," said George.

"What are we waiting for?" said Lockerbie.

"Cookies!" said Judy. "A whole lot of them!"

"Okay," said George. "Here is the plan. Lockerbie and I will find the butler's bottle, while everyone else bakes cookies."

"While you're out there, grab more wood," said Judy. "The stove needs to stay good and hot."

Lockerbie jumped from the bed and led the way.

Chapter 24

George followed Lockerbie out the front door with a small garden trowel he had found in the basement. They would've gone out the back, but they didn't want to disturb the nine little goblins. No one was sure how long the mincemeat would keep them asleep.

"This tree was just a sapling back then," said Lockerbie, once they reached the poplar tree.

It was now the largest of all the trees lining the edge of the property against the alley that ran behind the museum. Light from a security lamp filtered through the limbs to the ground where George would be digging.

"Hopefully the roots haven't crushed the bottle by now," said Lockerbie.

George hoped that Lockerbie was right. If the bottle was crushed, there was no way he could trap the Squidgicum Squee with it.

"Right here," said Lockerbie, using a paw to point to the spot. "Shouldn't be too far down, so be careful."

George took the trowel and dug into the first layer of soil past the grass. He tossed the grass aside and gently went a few inches deeper. Luckily, the dirt wasn't too hard because the recent storm had soaked the ground. The moist soil made the digging pretty simple.

George dug down about six more inches but still hadn't struck anything made out of glass. However, he did notice an occasional earthworm.

"Are you sure this is the right spot," said George. "Maybe…"

"I'm certain," said Lockerbie. "Just a few more inches down."

George continued to dig. The smell of dirt was stuck in his nose and his hands were completely covered in mud. Just as he released a sigh of frustration, the trowel struck something hard.

A wave of excitement filled George's body. "I think I found it," he said, using his hands to scoop away more dirt from the hard object. A glimpse of blue glass sparkled in the light.

"I told you so," said Lockerbie. Not only had she recovered from her sadness, her sassy attitude was back also.

George used the trowel to dig around the bottle, and within no time it was completely unearthed. They rushed it inside to wash it off.

"There's a big sink in the basement," said Judy, pulling another batch of cookies from the oven.

"Where's the wood?" said Granny.

"Forgot," said George. He was already headed through the breakfast room to the basement door. Lockerbie was close behind.

"I'll get it," said Violet.

In the basement, George quickly found the large sink. It was tucked inside a small area that Judy used as an office. He cranked the knobs on the faucet, releasing a steady stream of warm water. As the dirt washed away, George could see that something had been etched into the glass.

"Do you see that?" he asked Lockerbie.

She jumped to the edge of the sink and looked at the sparkling blue bottle. "Yes," said Lockerbie. "What does it say?"

George read the etching aloud to Lockerbie:

To Vacuum the S. Squee insert Ribbon of Lockerbie.
D. Ewing 1916

"I remember," said Lockerbie. "Ewing, the Butler tied this ribbon in my hair."

"Where did the ribbon come from?" asked George.

"He didn't tell me," said Lockerbie. "But he obviously charmed it."

"It was all part of his plan," said George.

"Maybe that's why I'm a ghost," said Lockerbie. "I'm not sure if I'm happy or mad about that!"

"Lockerbie," said George. "It is because of you that we can save Mr. Riley's poetry and the memories of my mother."

"I guess you're right," said Lockerbie. "My life and death have served a purpose. I can't be mad about that."

"Precisely," said George with a wink.

"Precisely," Lockerbie agreed.

As George looked at the clean and shiny-blue butler's bottle, he saw even more etchings, much fainter than the instructions. He quickly realized that the etchings were the names of his ancestors in their own handwriting. Some of them were only symbols, probably from those who were forbidden to read or write during slavery.

"Lockerbie," said George. "You're name is on the butler's bottle too - that makes you my family."

"It's certainly an honor," she said.

"What's going on down there?" Granny yelled from the basement door. "We need help with these cookies."

"Speaking of family," said Lockerbie.

"Duty calls," said George.

Chapter 25

Two-hundred and fifty mincemeat cookies later, the crew was finally finished. Judy divided them into four bags and handed them to everyone but Lockerbie.

"It's that time," said George. "We've got to go down the Goblin Hole. Is everyone in?"

Judy looked at the backdoor. "I wish I could lock it," she said. "But there's no use since the hinges are loose."

"Nothing evil will pass the brick dust," Granny reminded her. "Everything should be safe."

"That's right," said Judy. "Who needs to lock their doors when you have magic brick dust?"

"She's catching on." Granny nodded her head toward Judy but winked at George.

"To the Goblin hole!" said George.

"To the Goblin Hole," they all chimed back.

George completed a mental checklist of everything they would need. They had the cookies. The butler's bottle was in his backpack, and the charm bag was in his pocket.

"Granny," said George. "Did you give Judy her charm bag?"

"That's right," said Granny, pulling a small red flannel bag from her purse and handing it to Judy. "No goblin can bite you with this in your pocket."

"Why, thank you," said Judy. "Nobody wants a goblin bite!"

Once they made it downstairs, George and Violet removed the lid to the hole in the basement floor. The same warm glow that George saw before greeted them again.

"You all are crazy if you think I'm going to fit down that hole without breaking some bones," said Granny with a hand on her hip. "I'm no spring chicken."

"Violet and I will go first," said George. "Then you and Judy can roll on your stomachs and come down feet first. We'll grab your legs and ease you to the tunnel floor."

"I can't remember the last time I scooted anywhere on my stomach," said Granny, laughing nervously.

"Only to find missing socks that the cats drag under my bed," said Judy. "But we can do it, Betty."

"If you say so, my friend," said Granny.

Lockerbie was the first down the hole. When she reported that the coast was clear, George and Violet hopped down. Judy passed down the cookies and George's backpack. And just as George had prescribed, Judy and Granny came down on their stomachs.

"That wasn't so hard, was it?" said George.

Judy's hair was a mess, and Granny's wasn't much better. They both patted the dust off their clothes and pulled themselves together.

"What doesn't kill you, makes you stronger," said Judy.

"Ain't that the truth," said Granny. A smirk appeared on her face, letting George know that they were good to go.

George let Violet lead the way, since they were officially in her world. He was pretty sure he could remember how to get to the Goblin King's lair, but having a trustworthy guide this time was quite nice.

Just as they turned the corner from Lockerbie Street onto East Street, they had their first opportunity to test the cookies on some goblins.

"Quick," said Lockerbie. "There's more!"

Violet threw three and George threw even more. The goblins gobbled them just as fast as they caught them.

"Looks like this is going to work," said George.

Just as he spoke those words he noticed Violet still had a cookie in her hand, and it was headed towards her mouth.

"Violet," shouted George. "Stop!"

Violet shook her head and dropped the cookie on the floor. "I'm not so sure it's a good idea that I hold these," she said, handing the sack to George. "The temptation is too strong, and I'll be asleep with the rest of them."

"Well, that certainly won't do," said Lockerbie. "We need you awake and alert."

"I didn't even think of that," said Judy. "I almost forgot our little friend Violet was a goblin."

"Me, too," said Granny.

"I'm very much a goblin," said Violet. "And the smell of

those cookies is irresistible."

George and Violet devised a plan. When goblins approached, she would shout out their direction, and George would throw the cookies. This way, Violet could dodge her own mincemeat temptations.

They turned left onto Vermont Street and headed toward Pennsylvania Street. The torches seemed to be less bright this time around, and just as George began to wonder why, the torches suddenly blew out.

"That's never good," said Judy.

"King Spurlock must know you're here," said Violet. "But don't worry; I can navigate these tunnels with my eyes closed."

"No need to do that," said Lockerbie, taking the lead.

Somehow she had made herself brighter. George realized he wouldn't need to pull the flashlight from his backpack with Lockerbie's ghostly glow.

"How did you do that?" whispered Granny.

"Since you aren't a ghost, it would be very hard to explain," said Lockerbie.

"And I don't plan on becoming a ghost anytime soon," replied Granny. "So we better quiet down and get this whole thing over with."

George could tell that Granny was a bit spooked, but they pressed forward and followed Lockerbie's glow. Soon they turned north onto Pennsylvania. Just a few blocks ahead would be the hole leading to the lair beneath the Indianapolis Central Library.

Chapter 26

"Here it is," said Violet, standing before a dark hole in the tunnel's floor. "Be careful or you might fall through."

George remembered this hole very well, but when the Goblin King had led them there, it was illuminated by torchlight. Now, they were depending on Lockerbie's light.

"Lockerbie, can you go first?" asked George. "That way we can see our way down the ladder."

"Thank you, Lord," whispered Granny. "There's a ladder this time."

George giggled, even though his nerves were frayed. The last time he had gone down those stairs into the Goblin King's lair he was locked in a jail cell. He hoped that the butler's bottle would work, and that they could grab the Squidgicum Squee and leave.

Lockerbie illuminated the way as she floated down the ladder. George was right behind her, and when the smell of pickles hit his nose, he looked up and was face to face with a horde of goblins.

"Cookies!" yelped Lockerbie.

In desperation, George threw his whole bag of cookies at the goblins and rushed back up the ladder. He expected to feel sharp claws grab his leg, but he felt the heat of the charm bag instead. A few seconds later, the sounds of the gurgling and grunting goblins turned into snores.

"That was way too close," said Lockerbie.

"King Spurlock predicted that we would come this way," said Violet. "But I know a secret elevator he uses for stealing books from the library."

With Lockerbie's glow, Violet led them about a hundred feet further up Pennsylvania Street to 9th Street. Just a few steps down 9th street, they quickly turned down a narrow corridor. At the end was an arched, wooden door that looked like it belonged to a castle. Violet reached up and pulled a rope. The door split in the middle and opened just like an ordinary elevator.

"Come inside," she said.

"Not a fan of elevators," said Granny. "This looks like a trap."

"Hold my hand, Betty," said Judy. "We'll go together."

Lockerbie entered first and declared the elevator goblin-free. Once everyone else was inside, the doors slid shut. Violet pulled a lever that activated a rope and pulley system, and before they knew it, the elevator had lurched downward. George could hear Granny quietly humming to distract herself.

When the elevator stopped, Violet put a finger to her mouth. The doors slid open to a corridor lit with torches. The booming sound of the Goblin King's voice could be heard echoing against the stone walls.

"This way," whispered Violet.

They crept down the corridor, trying not to make a single sound, but the intense smell of vinegar got caught in George's nose, causing him to sneeze. Luckily, he trapped the sound in the crook of his arm. With an odor that strong, George worried that the goblins would outnumber the mincemeat cookies, but it was too late change course now.

The corridor opened to the back side of the lair - the opposite side of the stairs that George and Lockerbie had used before. Violet peeked around the corner and waved for George to come and take a look.

The site before him created a basketball-sized knot in his stomach. The Goblin King was holding Mr. Riley's top hat in one hand and the handkerchief in the other. Fortunately, the Book sat on a stone, undisturbed.

Sitting before the Goblin King was a congregation of at least a hundred goblins. And on the edges of the crowd were piles and piles of books, ready to be thrown to the Squidgicum Squee. The humidor was at the Goblin King's feet.

George quickly unzipped his backpack and pulled out the butler's bottle. It glistened in the torchlight. He could also feel the charm bag heating his thigh through his pocket.

"What do you see?" whispered Judy.

"Get the cookies ready," he said. "We'll need every single one of them."

Just then, the Goblin King's voice boomed even louder. Lockerbie growled.

"What language is that?" asked Granny.

"An ancient goblin language only used for magic," said Violet. "He is reversing the spell."

George couldn't hold himself back. He leapt out from behind the wall and screamed at the top of his lungs, "STOP!"

The goblins stood to their feet, but the Goblin King didn't stop speaking. A string of strange words continued to flow from his mouth.

"We got here too late," said Violet, coming to George's side. "The reversal is finished."

The Goblin King released a maniacal laugh as he put Mr. Riley's hat on his own head and waved the handkerchief in the air. When he finally stopped laughing, he turned and faced George. "We've been expecting you, Mr. Ewing."

"We've been expecting you, Mr. Ewing," the congregation of goblins repeated. Then, they lunged toward George and his crew.

"Hurry," said George. "Throw cookies! Fast!"

Judy flung her cookies off to the side of the goblins. As soon as the scent of mincemeat hit the air, the goblins stopped in their tracks and lifted their noses. Granny took the corner of her bag and flung it toward the center of the horde. Cookies went everywhere, and the goblins darted in every direction to find them.

"GET THEM, YOU FOOLS!" screamed the Goblin King. "NOT THE MINCEMEAT!"

So far, their plan was working, and in less than a minute the entire horde of goblins was fast asleep, except a few. And one of them was airborne and about to land on Judy.

"Judy," Granny yelled. "Look up!"

In a split second, Judy reached into her blazer pocket and pulled out one last cookie. She wound up her arm and launched it faster than the pitcher of the Indianapolis Indians. The goblin caught the cookie in his mouth and was asleep before he hit the ground. PLOP!

"Always keep a spare," she said, brushing the pretend dust from her shoulder pads.

But their sense of success quickly faded as the ground began to shake and rumble. Sharp stalactites fell from the cavern's ceiling, one nearly hitting George in the head.

"The old mincemeat trick!" the Goblin King roared. "Doesn't matter because you are too late." With that, his sinister laughing continued.

George could see a bright green sliver of light coming from the humidor, and as it opened, the shaking and rumbling got worse.

"The spell is broken," Granny yelled.

Lockerbie hopped over fallen stalactites and stood next to George. "The Squidgicum Squee is out!" she yelled. "We must follow the plan, George!"

The blob that oozed from the humidor could only be described as a milky green gelatin. It bubbled out onto the stone slab. As the Squidgicum Squee began to take better shape, the rumbling stopped. For a few moments everything was quiet. Then, two bullfrog looking eyes popped out of the jiggly mass, along with a mouth as wide a dinner plate.

"Let's see here," said King Spurlock. "I don't think we'll need this anymore!" He took Mr. Riley's hat from his head and tossed it inside the wide mouth of the Squidgicum Squee.

"No!" yelled Lockerbie.

"You're EVIL," shouted Judy.

"Bully!" added Granny.

George held the butler's bottle tightly in his hand, and he could feel the charm bag growing from warm to very hot. This gave George an idea. He quickly took the charm bag from his pocket and threw it at the Squidgicum Squee. It was swallowed like a muffin crumb.

"Take that!" George shouted.

The Squidgicum Squee jiggled back and forth, releasing several gaseous grunts. After a long pause, it BELCHED. Mr. Riley's hat flew from its mouth, landing smack dab on top of George's baseball cap.

"What did you do!" shouted the Goblin King.

At that moment, loud footsteps came charging down the staircase on the other side of the lair.

"More goblins," Lockerbie shrieked.

"No more cookies!" shouted Judy!

"I've got brick dust," exclaimed Granny, pulling the pouch from her purse. As fast as she could, she began drawing a thin circle. "Everyone, get inside!"

They followed Granny's instructions but realized that Violet was no longer with them.

"Where's Violet?" said George.

"She must've eaten a cookie," said Judy, pointing to the only sleeping goblin in a polka dotted dress.

"Dear lord!" said Granny.

By now the goblins had them surrounded, but they couldn't penetrate the circle. There were at least twenty-five of them.

"Anymore tricks up your sleeve?" shouted the Goblin King.

"Wouldn't you like to know!" George shouted back.

"Well, then," said the Goblin King. "I better get to work."

He hopped down from the stone slab and grabbed a stack of books. George, Judy, Granny, and Lockerbie froze and watched with horror. The goblins surrounded them and jumped up and down with glee.

"Gold! Gold! Gold!" they shouted.

And just like that, the Goblin King fed the Squidgicum Squee a book. Whatever book it was, George knew it had just been erased from history. The Squidgicum Squee swallowed it down in a simple gulp. It jiggled back and forth for a few moments and then released a loud belch. A puff of gold dust sparkled down to the slab. A goblin jumped up and quickly swept it into an iron pot.

George turned to Lockerbie. "I need your ribbon," he said.

"Take it," said Lockerbie. "It's yours."

George reached down and took the pink ribbon from between Lockerbie's ears and pushed it into the bottle. Instantly, the bottle flickered with blue light.

"Back off!" George yelled to the goblins surrounding them. "Or I'll suck you into this bottle like a genie to a lamp."

The bottle's light brightened to a radiant blue. The goblins took a step back and parted ways. George stepped out of the circle.

"STOP!" he shouted at the Goblin King, who was just about to throw another book to the Squidgicum Squee. George recognized the cover immediately – *Charlotte's Web*.

"Or what?" spat the Goblin King. "That fancy-schmancy bottle doesn't scare me."

The bottle turned ice cold in George's hands and began to hum as if air was blowing into it. He stepped closer to the Squidgicum Squee and aimed the bottle directly at it.

"Intention!" yelled Granny. "That's how magic works!"

George thought of his mother and all the books she had read to him. He imagined what it would be like if those memories of her were instantly gone with the books thrown into the Squidgicum Squee. His happiest memories of his mother would be gone forever. George would NOT let that happen, and the butler's bottle seemed to respond to these emotions. It grew even colder, and the humming grew louder.

From the corners of his eyes, George could see the Goblin King's face turn from curiosity to terror. He dropped the copy of *Charlotte's Web* and leapt into the air towards George. As the Goblin King reached out his hands to snatch the bottle, George instantaneously whipped the bottle around and aimed it at the Goblin King's face. A stream of grey fog swirled out of the bottle and twisted itself around the Goblin King. As it raised him into the air, it whirled around faster and faster like a small, yet mighty tornado. And as fast as it shot out from the bottle, it reeled itself in, including the Goblin King. He was gone. Only a small scream wafted out of the bottle and into the air.

Lockerbie barked wildly. Granny and Judy cheered. The remaining goblins retreated into the dark corners of the cavern.

Chapter 27

"I wasn't expecting that," said Judy. "I figured we'd be dealing with the Goblin King for another hundred years."

"Good grief, Judy" said Lockerbie. "It would be your ghost next!"

"I don't know whose ghost it's going to be, but somebody better take care of Mr. Jello-Pudding over there," said Granny, nudging George with her elbow. "We're not through yet."

George walked closer to the Squidgicum Squee and gave

it a closer look. "Do you talk?" asked George. "Or are you just a big silent eraser?"

The Squidgicum Squee jiggled back and forth and made some gurgling sounds. Its large yellow eyes opened wider as if it were trying to get a better look at George. Two nostrils emerged from the folds of slime between its eyes and mouth. It seemed to be sniffing George to see what he was made of. Then, with no warning, its mouth flew open.

"Get back!" shouted Lockerbie. "It will swallow you!"

But George wasn't so sure. The mouth opened wider and wider until it was so wide that George thought it couldn't open any further. But it did.

"It's swallowing itself," said Judy, placing a hand over her mouth.

"Would you look at that?" said Granny. "I've never seen anything like it."

Judy was right. In the blink of an eye, the Squidgicum Squee's mouth snapped backwards, and the whole gelatinous creature vanished.

"It's gone," said Lockerbie.

"But look!" said George. "The charm bag!"

On the slab where the Squidgicum Squee once sat, was the little, red charm bag that George had thrown to get Mr. Riley's hat back – the hat that was still nested on top of his baseball cap. George picked up the little bag, but he could tell that something was very different about it. He untied the cotton string and emptied the contents into his hand.

"A diamond ring!" said George.

"A diamond ring, really?" said Judy.

"Let me see that?" said Granny.

George held out his hand. Granny walked over and looked at the sparkling diamond ring. She clasped her hands over her heart. Tears rolled down her face.

"It's your wedding ring, isn't it?" said George, handing

the ring to Granny.

Granny nodded and took the ring from George's hand. She slid it onto her finger. "I'm going to be okay," she said, taking a deep breath. "I'm going to be okay."

"It was the rose petal," said George.

"True love," said Granny.

Judy walked over and placed a hand on Granny's arm. "Miracles do happen," she said.

"When I lost this ring, I also lost myself," said Granny. "But now I'm found."

"Amazing Grace," said Judy.

Granny began to hum and then to sing. George and Judy joined her.

Amazing grace! How sweet the sound
That saved a wretch like me!
I once was lost, but now am found;
Was blind, but now I see.

George took off Mr. Riley's hat and pulled the handkerchief from the inside. "Here, Granny," he said. "Has a little blood on it, but it'll dry your tears."

Granny gave George a wink, and took the handkerchief. When he turned around, Goblins had them surrounded.

George quickly grabbed the butler's bottle which was resting at his feet. He spun around and aimed it at the goblins. But something had changed about them, too. They weren't drooling for gold or revenge. In fact, instead of rushing at him, they all bent down on one knee.

"King Ewing!" one shouted.

"Oh, I don't think so," said George. "But I know somebody qualified for the job."

He walked over to Violet, who was still asleep on the floor. "Judy," he said. "Do you happen to have a pickle in your pocket?"

Judy fumbled around in her blazer pocket, and pulled out a small gherkin. "Always keep a spare," she said with a wink as she threw the pickle to George.

It only took a few swipes of the pickle under Violets nose to wake her. "What? What? What happened?" she said fumbling to her feet. "Where's King Spurlock?"

George held up the butler's bottle. "The Goblin King is in this bottle," said George. "But the Goblin Queen is standing right in front of me."

"Wh-wh-what?" Violet stuttered.

George turned to face the goblins. "Violet, the Queen of Goblins!" he shouted. "Follow her command, or meet the same fate as Spurlock!"

Granny held the bottle in the air. One goblin stood before the others and stomped his foot three times, "All hale Queen Violet!" he shouted.

Another goblin stood and stomped her foot three times. "All hale Queen Violet," she shouted.

The rest of the goblins stood and stomped three times. "All hale Queen Violet," they cheered.

Violet quickly patted her dress free of wrinkles. She stood up straight and shouted, "First order of business! Return all books to the library!"

The goblins immediately obeyed her commands and began hauling the piles of books away.

"Queen Violet," said George. "It looks like you have a faithful crew."

"Thanks to you," she said, blushing.

"No," said George. "Thanks to you."

"Looks like a lot is going to change around this place," said Granny.

"You've got that right," said Judy.

Lockerbie didn't say anything. In fact, it looked as if she

was beginning to fade again.

"What's wrong, Lockerbie?" said George.

"My business is finished," she said. "My spirit is calling me to Crown Hill."

George's heart sank. He forgot all about that. With Spurlock and the Squidgicum Squee gone, Lockerbie didn't have to guard Mr. Riley's room anymore. "But you can still visit, can't you?"

"Yes," said Lockerbie, "and I will very often."

"Oh, Lockerbie," said Judy, "the museum will never be the same without you. Who am I going to talk to? Who is going to love the house as much as you and I do?"

"Me," said Granny, putting her arm around Judy. "Are you taking applications?"

Judy gave Granny a stunned look that quickly turned into a smile. "You're hired," she said. "I'll pick you up every morning."

"You just got a job," said George with a big grin.

"Movin' and shakin', that's how we make bacon," Granny said, swaying her hips.

"Would you all like a ride to Crown Hill," said Violet. "Now that I'm Queen, I have special access to the Goot."

"What is that, exactly?" asked Lockerbie.

"The Goot is the goblin's water trolley system," she explained. "It was used only by Spurlock and his servants."

"Sounds quite interesting," said Judy.

"I don't know about this Goot business," said Granny.

"I guess we could walk the four miles to Crown Hill," said George.

"Fine, but if I fall overboard," said Granny, "I can't swim."

George glanced at Lockerbie. Her light had faded even more. "You'll be fine, Granny," he said. "Now, let's take Lockerbie to Crown Hill.

Chapter 28

The Goot resembled a small steamboat. It was even powered by a large paddle wheel in the back with the captain's helm in the very center. A short, stocky goblin with a captain's hat met them at the gangplank.

"Queen Violet," he croaked. "Where can I take you and your servants?"

"Excuse me?" said Granny, planting a hand firmly on her hip.

"These are not my servants," said Violet. Her green skin turned a bit red. "They are my friends, and we would like to go to Crown Hill Cemetery."

"Kitchen's Mausoleum! All aboard!" said the Goblin. "Captain Snoop, at your service."

Everyone boarded the Goot and took seats on the wooden benches at the boat's front, except Violet. A large and golden throne was reserved for her in the middle. "This will be hard to get used to," she said. "I don't feel at all like a Queen."

"And that is why you'll be a great queen," said Lockerbie, perching herself at the very tip of the boat like an ornamental mermaid. Even though she was right there, her voice was beginning to sound more distant.

The boat's paddle began chopping the water, and in no time at all, they were chugging down the canal. Just like the tunnels, the canal had stone walls and was lit by torchlight. What George didn't expect was the music coming from small pipes on top of the captain's helm.

"Would you listen to that," said Judy. "This little steamship even has a calliope."

The music was a jolly little tune that reminded George of a carnival ride. It also made the trip down the canal go by very quickly.

"Kitchen's Mausoleum," hollered Captain Snoop. "Queen Violet, the Goot will await your return."

Violet led everyone off the boat and down a narrow hallway to a set of stairs. At the top of the stairs was another arched wooden door.

"Is this another one of those rickety elevators?" said Granny.

"This time we'll be going up instead of down," said Violet. "This elevator will take us to the inside of Kitchen's Mausoleum."

"What have I gotten myself into?" Granny said, shaking her head.

"I know where we're going," said George. "Dad showed me this mausoleum once. Isn't it built into the side of a hill?"

Violet pulled a rope, and the door split in two. "That's the one," she said. "Goblins have been using it to access the cemetery for over a century."

Inside the elevator, Violet pulled a lever to activate the rope and pulley system. The small car lurched upward toward the surface.

Once again, George heard Granny humming. This time, he hummed too. When the doors opened into the mausoleum, Lockerbie was the first to exit.

It was completely dark inside the mausoleum, except for Lockerbie's very faint glow. With Mr. Riley's hat still on his head, he had to duck from hitting the low ceiling.

"What's that?" said Granny.

George took off his backpack and unzipped it. Next to some books, he found his flashlight. He grabbed it and flipped it on. He shined its narrow beam towards Granny's voice.

"Looks like you bumped into Mr. Kitchen's tomb," said George.

"Don't tell me there's a coffin in there?" said Granny.

George couldn't help but laugh at his grandma. She was the strongest woman he knew, but she was easily spooked.

"You best get me outa this place," she said.

"Shine your light this way," said Violet. "This door leads to the outside, but I can't find the deadbolt."

George shined his light toward Violet. "There it is," he said.

Violet clicked the deadbolt to the left and pushed on the heavy cement door. As a gust of wind blew into the mausoleum, Granny pushed her way to the front. She was the first one out.

"Next time I'm in a grave," she said, "I best be dead."
George giggled.

"Don't snicker at me, boy," said Granny, "or I'll haunt your pants off when I die. I won't be one of those nice ghosts like Lockerbie."

"Speaking of Lockerbie..." said Violet.

Judy was already following Lockerbie up the hill. As the rest of them caught up, George looked down at his watch. It was almost 3:00am.

The wind had really picked up, tossing grass clippings and leaves through the rows of gravestones. And on the wind, came a voice. "Lockerbie? Lockerbie? Where are you my little girl?"

Judy stopped in her tracks. Lockerbie's tail began to wag. She looked back as Judy knelt down on her knees. The little white poodle rushed over and gave her a few licks on the cheek. "It's him, isn't it?" said Judy.

"I'm going home," said Lockerbie, her tail wagging even faster.

"I'll miss you, my sweet little friend," said Judy, beginning to cry.

"Don't cry," said Lockerbie. "I'll come back to Mr. Riley's room. You'll know when I'm there."

"Okay." Judy wiped the tears from her eyes. "Tell Mr. Riley that his poetry is safe with us."

Lockerbie turned toward the hill and began trotting away. George and everyone else slowly walked behind her. And then, when they reached a vantage point where they could see the top of Crown Hill, a man stood there with the same kind of light as Lockerbie. He wore a top hat and carried a cane.

"Poodle girl!" he called. "There you are."

With that, Lockerbie's prance turned into a run. She bolted up the hill and into Mr. Riley's arms. He held her and cuddled her for a few minutes and then peered down the hill. He propped his cane against one leg and took off his hat and waved it in the air. And as he waved, he and Lockerbie slowly disappeared.

George gathered Granny and their new friends into a hug.

"Together again," said Judy. "The way it should be."

"The way it should be," said George.

"That's right," said Granny.

Chapter 29

George woke up to the smell of biscuits and gravy. He rolled out of bed and headed downstairs where he found Granny in front of the stove in her blue and yellow Monday housecoat.

"Your dad should be here any minute," she said. "He called me from his taxi."

George sat down at the kitchen table and wondered how they were going to explain everything to his dad. Granny must have been thinking the same thing.

"Your dad ain't going to believe what happened to us,"

she said.

"I think he'll be more surprised that you left the house," said George.

Granny's left arm rested at her side while she mixed the gravy with her right one. Her diamond ring sparkled in the light from the kitchen window.

At that moment, the front door burst open. "I'm home!" Mr. Ewing shouted.

George and Granny stopped what they were doing and rushed into the living room to give Mr. Ewing some love.

"Who's the lady in the Cadillac parked in our driveway?" he asked.

"It's Monday!" shouted Granny with a panicked look crossing her face. "I've got to go to work!"

"Work?" said Mr. Ewing. The look on his face showed obvious bewilderment.

"Maybe Judy has time for breakfast," said George.

"Who is Judy?" asked Mr. Ewing.

"Well, tell her to come inside," Granny told George. "She's probably wondering what the problem is."

George ran outside and tapped on Judy's window. She was in the middle of opening a giant bag of what looked like peanuts. She finally rolled down the window.

"Are those peanuts?" asked George.

"For the squirrels at museum," said Judy. "I like to keep peanuts in my pocket to feed them when I see them in the yard."

"Better peanuts than pickles," said George.

"Isn't that the truth?"

"Hey," said George. "Granny was hoping you could come inside for a quick breakfast before work. She's making biscuits and gravy."

Judy switched the ignition and pulled out the key. "I'd love some," she said. "I haven't had good biscuits and gravy in years."

"You'll get to meet my dad too," said George, opening Judy's door for her.

Inside, a place setting was already made for Judy. Mr. Ewing had taken over the cooking, while Granny dressed for work.

"Welcome to our home, Ms. Hatfield," said Mr. Ewing. "I hear you all got yourselves into a pickle while I was gone."

George laughed at his dad's choice of words.

"Will you have time to tell me about it over breakfast?" he continued.

Granny walked into the kitchen, wearing a pink blouse with tan slacks. "It's a twisted tale," she said. "Your son had me romping around in graveyards and talking to ghosts and goblins..."

"Goblins!" laughed Mr. Ewing.

"She's not joking," said George. "Remember the little green girl you saw while mowing..."

"You've got to be kidding," said Mr. Ewing, shaking his head.

"Everybody, sit down," said Granny.

Mr. Ewing placed the hot biscuits and gravy on the kitchen table, while Granny poured herself and Judy some hot coffee.

"George," said Granny, "tell it from the start."

Ewing Family Snickerdoodles

1 cup butter
1 ½ cup sugar
2 eggs
2 ¾ cup flour
2 tsp cream of tartar
1 tsp baking soda
½ tsp salt

Cream together the butter and sugar. Mix in the eggs. In a separate bowl, mix together the flour, cream of tartar, baking soda and salt. Gradually blend the two mixtures together. Roll into one inch balls. Roll balls into a blend of sugar and cinnamon. Bake on slightly greased cookie sheets at 350 degrees for 8 minutes.

Enjoy!

ACKNOWLEDGEMENTS

I would like to thank the historians at the James Whitcomb Riley Museum Home: Jim Obergfell, Chris Mize, Jim Bishop, and the REAL Judy Hatfield. Because of you, James Whitcomb Riley's legacy continues to inspire countless individuals every day. I would also like to thank Judy Hatfield and Vivian Morehous for critiquing and editing the drafts of this book. And finally, I would like to thank everyone who contributes to the Riley Foundation for Children: the doctors, nurses, hospital staff, foundation staff, Board of Governors, teachers, students, parents, patients and ALL the donors who give their time and resources. Thank you!

Professor Watermelon

GEORGE AND THE GOBLIN HOLE

George Ewing takes a tour of the James Whitcomb Riley Museum Home and realizes that he is the 5th great grandson of Mr. Riley's butler. Even more surprisingly, he uncovers a magical plot that he must finish. For a hundred years, the Squidgicum Squee, a creature that swallows and erases books from history, has been trapped in Mr. Riley's cigar box. But the Goblins have stolen it and plan to release it. Will George stop the Goblins in time before they carry out their wicked plan?

THE AUTHOR

Professor Watermelon (Chadwick Gillenwater) travels the country inspiring elementary students to use the written word as a joyful way of creative self-expression. As an experienced school librarian, storyteller, and children's author, Professor Watermelon has the tools to motivate his students to build characters, twist plots, and dream-up knew worlds. To learn more about Professor Watermelon and his creative writing classes, take a look at his website: www.professorwatermelon.com

THE ILLUSTRATOR

Mr. Smart lives in a bunker somewhere in Indiana where he is the resident cartoonist for the Indiana Pacers. He has also provided cartoons and illustrations for other NBA, WNBA, NHL, and NFL teams as well as Pepsi, Kroger, Hardee's, and Progressive Insurance. Not bad for living in a bunker! Illustrating children's books is Mr. Smart's passion, and he looks forward to creating many more books with Professor Watermelon. You can reach Mr. Smart at smartoonist@gmail.com

Made in the USA
Lexington, KY
02 August 2016